The Fall of Promise

(The Wolves of Promise Falls, Book 1)

T. S. JOYCE

The Fall of Promise

ISBN: 9798417823015
Copyright © 2022, T. S. Joyce
First electronic publication: February 2022

T. S. Joyce
www. tsjoyce.com

NOTE FROM THE AUTHOR:

This book is a work of fiction. The names, characters, places, and incidents are products of the writer's imagination or have been used fictitiously and are not to be construed as real. Any resemblance to persons, living or dead, actual events, locale or organizations is entirely coincidental. The author does not have any control over and does not assume any responsibility for third-party websites or their content.

Published in the United States of America

First digital publication: February 2022
First print publication: February 2022

DEDICATION

For the 1010 Crew.

ACKNOWLEDGMENTS

You readers have done more for me and my stories than I can even explain on this teeny page. You found my books, and ran with them, and every share, review, and comment makes release days so incredibly special to me.

1010 is magic and so are you.

ONE

"Choose one."

Denver Mosley frowned at the piece of paper her mother slid across the table. Three names were written onto it.

Aloud, she read, "Bartholomew Hanson, thirty-four years old, five foot nine, no kits, no prospects, willing to relocate, works as a foreman at Lancaster—Mom, what is this?"

"It's the three best matches your father and I have found for you."

Denver probably had about forty-five wrinkles on her forehead right now from her eyebrows trying to reach her hairline. "So, this is a menu of men?"

"Not just men. Fox shifters, like you."

"I'm aware of what I am," she said, standing. She shoved the paper back across the table. "I'm not choosing a mate off this list of strangers."

"You promised," her mom said in that calm tone Denver hated. It always made her feel like she was being a difficult child, but she wasn't a child anymore. She was thirty years old and completely capable of making her own life decisions.

"That wasn't a real promise."

"Yes, it was," her father said from where he was sitting at the head of the dining room table.

"I should've known this was some stupid ambush," she muttered. "We never sit in the formal dining room. Only bad stuff happens in here."

"You're being melodramatic," her father said. "Sit down."

"You can't be serious about a childhood

promise I made when I was eight years old," she said, sitting slowly. It was time to have a real discussion about this, because it was getting to be too much lately. "I'm fine. I'm happy."

"Are you?" Mom asked. "Because all we've seen for the last two years is you moping around."

Don't. Snap. "I haven't been moping. I've just been busy with work." Lie. "And a budding social life." Also a lie. "And, and...I'm thinking about moving!" Lie also, but she needed them to focus on anything other than her love life. "Far away. Maybe to Texas." To escape this stupid discussion.

Both of her parents had their heads cocked to the side, and the looks on their faces said they didn't believe a damn word she said.

"You turned thirty—"

"—two days ago—"

"And that was the deal. It's the same deal with every fox shifter," Dad pointed out. "You have until thirty to choose, and if you don't, the

5

parents get to step in."

"Well, Bart made it to thirty-four without his parents trying to set him up with a loveless match, so that means his parents are four years more awesome than you—"

"His parents are dead."

"—well…that's…a really sad story actually." She'd been ready to tirade, but that sucked the wind right out of her sails. "Why is he volunteering for this?"

"Because he understands the importance of breeding," Mom said in a tired tone.

Breeding. That's what every fox shifter aspired to do, right? None of the other parts of their lives were important, just the number of kits they could produce.

Mom shoved the paper back at her. "These three have no link to our lineage, and they are all adequate matches."

"I don't want to settle for adequate," she murmured. "I want something more."

Mom pointed to Bartholomew's name. "There

is nothing more important than this. Do you think your father and I were a love match? We weren't. We did our duty and agreed to our parents' wishes, and we had you and your brothers and sisters, who, I might point out, have already all paired up—"

"—even your younger siblings," she finished in sync with her mom. This wasn't the first time she'd gotten this speech. "You've picked apart everyone I've ever tried with," Denver uttered.

"Because none of them were good enough for you."

"But they were my choice."

"But they were human."

"So what?" she demanded. "I would still have kits. And I could've been happy."

Dad slammed his hand onto the table. "There aren't enough of us left, and you're not diluting the line with a human mate. You are the only one who doesn't understand that. How many parties have we thrown? How many meet-ups have we gone to where you ignore every good prospect so you can go run around town with humans? And even if that was a valid excuse, you haven't dated anyone in three years. You didn't try with anyone."

"Because you shame me for anyone I find interesting!"

Denver's phone lit up on the table, and she dragged her attention to the glowing screen. It was a text from her oldest sister, Lyndi. It was two words, but that tiny sentence sucked the fire right out of her.

He's back.

It was enough. Denver knew exactly what that meant.

Daylen was back.

Daylen, who had left without a word of goodbye two years ago.

Daylen, in line for the crown in the Sheridan Pack.

Daylen, the werewolf.

Daylen, the one she'd leaned on since she was six.

Daylen, her very best friend in the entire world.

Lyndi was always the last one to know anything, so how did she find out?

Denver slid her attention to her parents. "Daylen is back," she whispered in shock. "Did you know?"

Mom's lips tightened into a thin line, and she refused to answer. That was a yes.

Daylen was really back! Excitement trilled through her and she stood so fast the chair flew out from behind her. She grabbed her phone and bolted for the door, and yanked her jacket and purse off the bench sitting beside it.

"We aren't done with this discussion," her dad called behind her.

Daylen, Daylen, Daylen! Denver leapt off the porch and straight over all five stairs, landed hard in the snow, and sprinted for her beat-up old blue and silver Dodge.

"Please start, please start!" she chanted as she turned the key.

And it did! First try! It's like the universe wanted her to see him faster. She kissed the steering wheel and put her seatbelt on as quick as she could.

Her parents were standing on the porch, so she waved to them as she drove down their snowy driveway.

He's back.

She hadn't known how important those two tiny little words could be.

She hadn't been moping for the last two years, as her parents had put it.

Denver had just been missing her best friend.

TWO

Daylen felt nothing.

He tried to as he scanned the property that used to mean the world to him, but all that remained was numbness.

"Are you going to finish it?" Stark asked from behind him.

Oh, Daylen had heard him there. He'd smelled him, too, but if Stark wanted to kill him, he would've already done it.

"I don't know," Daylen answered honestly as he shifted his weight in the snow in front of the old miner's cabin he'd vowed to fix up.

Stark came to stand beside him. He'd shaved the sides of his hair and pulled the blond mohawk into a knot at the back. He looked different. "You gonna go in?" he asked.

"Workin' up to it."

"Want to talk?" Stark wore a baiting smile. They weren't friends.

"Fuck you."

"Mmm," Stark said, a snarl in his throat. "Tessa sent me here with a message."

"If my mother had something to say, she would give me the message herself. What do you want?"

"To see your face when you find out."

Daylen inhaled deeply. Why couldn't he feel anything? "Find out what?"

"Most of the Pack left."

Daylen jerked his gaze to Stark. "What? Who left?"

"It'll be easier if I list the ones who stayed. Tessa, you, Marsden..." The grin that took Stark's face was evil. "...and me."

Ten wolves. Ten wolves had left. Ten layers of protection had abandoned them, and he couldn't really blame them. Not after what he and Tessa had done. Not after what had happened in the mountains of Montana with Krome's Crew. Not after what happened with Ruby Daughtry.

"Aw, poor prince of the Sheridan Pack. There's no kingdom left to inherit." The joy that vibrated from Stark was a weight in his chest, like Daylen had swallowed cement.

"Why did you stay?" Daylen asked.

"Two reasons. One, where would I go? Huh? We both know this is my last-chance Pack. I'm stuck, but I'm okay with that."

Numb, numb, numb. The wolf inside of him might as well not even exist right now. "What's the second reason?"

Stark's lips curled back and exposed his sharp canines, and his piercing blue eyes blazed almost white. Voice low, he snarled, "I wouldn't miss your downfall for the fuckin' world."

Daylen let the venom in Stark's voice coat his skin like tar. He blinked tiredly at the dilapidated miner's cabin as Stark's boot steps faded away.

"Wolf," he murmured softly to the sleeping animal inside of him. "Are you there?"

No answer. This was the first time he'd passed on a chance to fight Stark. Honestly, Daylen couldn't be angry with what was happening to him, because he deserved this.

It was the universe's way of setting things right, because he'd done something horrible.

Daylen stepped up to the door and rested his hand on the handle. Next to it was a dog bed, half covered in snow, which made no sense. Dogs weren't allowed in his territory. The wolf would eat them. It had been two years since he'd marked these woods though. Perhaps, the woods had forgotten who he was.

Daylen dug in his pocket for the house key, but he didn't need it. The breeze pushed the door open before he could even get the key in the slot. *Creeeeak.*

Inside, natural light filtered through the windows. The light switch didn't work, but that was probably because he quit paying the power bill a couple years ago. That's when his mom, and Alpha, Tessa had pulled the entire Pack to Montana because his brother, Vager, had been transferred there to serve three years of his murder sentence.

Everything had gone wrong, and the tornado of what happened to the Pack over the last few months had made him block this place out entirely. He'd had to. There had been no room for looking back or missing happy places.

His breath froze in front of his face as he stepped inside. The wolf might be quiet inside of him, but he still had all the heightened senses.

There were yellow linen curtains on the windows, and the kitchen cabinets had new, matching pine doors. There was a rug under the table, which had been righted by someone after he'd destroyed everything in here the night he'd found out about Vager's sentencing. Only two of the chairs had survived him, but the broken ones had been replaced by a pair of white ones. There was a vase of old, dead, dried-out flowers on the table, and in the corner of the living room, by the wood burning stove, was a pile of blankets and a pillow.

Someone had been squatting here.

The hairs rose on the back of his neck and he scented the air, but all he smelled was old cabin and cold. Whoever had been here had left long ago.

Something fluttered on the small kitchen countertop, and he jerked his attention to a folded piece of yellow, ruled notebook paper, held in place by a rock. The window over the old, rusted kitchen sink was broken, and snow had fallen over the counter. The breeze was lifting the corner of that letter.

Daylen's boots made hollow sounds across the aged, scuffed wooden floors. Gingerly, he picked up the letter.

Day,

Where did you go?

Denver

Daylen dropped the letter like he'd been burned.

He'd abandoned her, and that loyal little fox had still come here and cleaned up the mess he left behind.

This was the part he hadn't been ready for.

Shaking his head, he backed away from the letter as he watched it flutter to the floor in the breeze.

No. No, no, no, he couldn't do this yet.

There was a grenade in his chest, and the only thing that could put the pin back in it was an escape from this place.

He'd been happy here, and now that would never be his story again. No one was to blame but him, because there was a shadow that would follow him for always now.

He'd been happy, and then everything had

gotten yanked away, and he'd allowed it.

And worse than that...he'd participated in a destiny he'd seen coming from a mile away, and hadn't even lifted a finger to stop it.

He'd done something unforgiveable, and this place was no longer a home.

It was just a reminder of all that he'd burned to the ground.

THREE

He wasn't here.

Denver scanned the living room of Daylen's cabin and her eyes landed on the note she'd written, drifting slowly across the floor as the breeze through the broken windowpane picked up and then died off again.

It smelled like him in here...kind of. Like him, but different than she remembered.

He'd read her note, so why hadn't he texted her with a *Hey, you wanna meet at Quincy's Steakhouse to catch up?*

She checked her phone and opened his text

thread, but nope. There were just her forty-seven unanswered messages over the last two years.

She didn't understand what she'd done in the first place to make him so angry that he would leave her like that with no explanation.

Part of her had feared him dead, even though her family had explained to her ninety different times that sometimes werewolf Packs picked up and moved off for no known reason, because they were crazy. All shifters knew werewolves were crazy, except for her, apparently.

Denver moved to shove her phone into her back pocket, but it buzzed with a text. A feeling of such hope bloomed in her heart as she jerked the phone back up in front of her face.

It wasn't him. It wasn't Daylen.

It was Mom sending her a photo of the stupid mate menu.

And then another picture, zoomed in on Bartholomew's information. Her parents clearly had a preference.

The breeze from the broken window lifted

that old letter into a little tornado at her feet before it settled again. *Where did you go?* It had been months since she'd been here, at least in this form. Sometimes when she Changed into her fox, she still ended up here in Daylen's woods. On those nights, she'd slept on the dog bed she'd dragged to the front door. She didn't know why her animal liked coming back here. Perhaps it was a link to a time where everything made sense, and the fox didn't want to let go of it yet.

Werewolves were crazy, and foxes were loyal.

Stupid boy.

She was going to find Daylen and make him explain himself, and then she would take him out to Quincy's Steakhouse and get him a good steak and make him spill his guts and everything would go back to normal.

God, she needed everything to go back to normal.

Okay. Okay!

If he wasn't here, he would be at one of his

21

favorite places. That wolf was a creature of habit, and she knew a thing or two about tracking.

She would find him, and everything would be all right.

It had to be, because they were best friends.

As she zoomed down the overgrown dirt road and back to the main, she compiled a list of places to search in her head, and the order to search them.

First up was Promise Falls, where they'd spent every summer swinging off a rope swing into the river. It had a bench there he used to go sit on for hours when he had something on his mind. The bench, however, was empty, and someone had carved a wiener into the spot where she used to sit with Daylen, so she pulled out her pocket knife and took ten minutes to turn the little cartoon carving into a horse. She wasn't sitting on some wooden dick when she and Daylen hung out here again. A horse was better.

Back in the truck she went, and she drove to

Poplar Street to see if she saw his truck parked in front of the bars they used to go together. Leadville, Colorado wasn't that big, and most of the buildings were historic buildings, but two of them were saloons turned bars. In a couple months, spring would be upon them and the road would be taken over by the farmer's market on Wednesdays, but today it was just her and a handful of townies cruising. He wasn't at the general store, he wasn't at the bars, and his truck wasn't parked anywhere near the main streets. Maybe he'd sold it. What if he was driving something new?

No. No! He wouldn't ever give up his 1985 light blue, two-door Chevy Silverado. He and his brother, Vager, had spent an entire summer fixing that old clunker up.

Think, Denver.

It was snowing, so he wouldn't be shooting hoops with his Pack up at the high school basketball courts. Fishing was out because it was too cold for much action. Maybe the old swingset at Fireman's Park!

She pulled a right off Poplar and sped off toward the park, if it could be called that anymore. It was old as sin and most of the playground equipment was dilapidated, and it was mostly a make-out spot for teens who were out past curfew now. She drove fifteen minutes to get to it and then pulled right up front. No one was there, and the swings she grew up on were swaying gently in the breeze like ghosts were on them.

She'd always loved the woods around this place, but ever since Daylen had disappeared, they had felt too empty for her to stay more than a few minutes.

He wouldn't be at his mom's. Daylen and Tessa Hoda had always had a strained relationship, and he was rarely at her place unless there was a Pack meeting. Wait, they had Pack meetings at different houses each time.

Ding, ding, ding. Of course he was probably at a Pack meeting! They had just gotten home and probably needed to dig back into setting up their old lives! Old jobs and old homes none of them had bothered to sell before they left. She knew, because she'd kept an eye on the real estate section of the Hometown News.

All the wolves lived within a five-mile radius of Tessa's house, so Denver aimed her truck for the mountains. She had about twenty-five miles worth of gas left, and that would be enough. Probably.

The drive to Walker's house was eternal, and when she reached it, her heart jumped up into her throat. Not because Daylen's truck was there, but because there was a for-sale sign in the yard. It looked crisp and clean and brand new, and the flyer canister attached to it was completely full. What the heck?

She threw her truck into park and jogged to the front door, knocked loudly, and waited. No answer. When she checked the carport, Walker's truck definitely wasn't there. His driveway only had one set of tire marks and some footprints leading to the for-sale sign and straight back to the car.

Okaaay.

She made her way to the next house. Bruce wasn't home either, and the same realtor sign and tire prints and boot prints were in the yard.

What the hell? What was happening?

Two more houses had the same fresh for-sale signs up, and Denver hit her hand on the steering wheel in frustration.

No more. She drove straight to Tessa's house, and there it was.

This was the last place she'd expected it to be, but there was the truck she'd been looking for.

Daylen's Silverado, Stark's Camaro, and a new Ford Bronco that was probably Tessa's were the only vehicles parked out front.

A fox shifter was nothing like a wolf shifter. A wolf was nothing like a fox. But this little fox had learned a long time ago that she should never psych herself out before visiting the wolves.

One deep breath, no fear, and she shoved the

door open and walked up that snowy walkway like she owned the place. Daylen had once told her that boldness was the only thing wolves respected. However, sometimes there was a fine line between boldness and stupidity, and this place smelled strongly like wolf markings. Somebody was reclaiming territory, and here Denver came, another predator into wolf territory like she didn't give a care about survival, but okay. She was still going to file this under boldness.

If she got eaten, at least she wouldn't have to marry Bartholomew.

The door was thrown open before she even lifted her hand to knock, and there was the devil herself. Tessa Hoda was Alpha of one of the biggest werewolf Packs in North America, and it wasn't surprising. Her dominance made her feel like she weighed a thousand pounds.

Her whiskey-colored eyes were lightened, and she didn't wear a stitch of makeup. Tessa had to be her parents' age, fifty at least, but she didn't look a day over forty. She looked different though. Her cheekbones were sharper, and her sandy brown hair wasn't curled. It laid lifeless at her shoulders.

"What do you want, fox?" Tessa growled.

"You know what I want," Denver said softly. "Can you tell him I'm here?"

"He knows you're here. He heard that shit-wagon coming from a mile away."

Denver frowned. If Daylen knew she was here, why hadn't he been the one to open the door?

"He just left—"

"We are going through some things here that don't concern you, fox," Tessa interrupted her. "It's probably safest for you if you leave."

"Day?" she called out.

"He can hear you just fine. He just doesn't want to see you," Tessa said, an edge to her voice that cut like a razor.

Denver dropped her gaze. "Vager's house is for sale."

"Listen to me," Tessa uttered low in a voice full of venom. "You won't poke around my Pack like you used to. You won't take anyone's focus, or fill anyone's head with little fox things." Tessa felt like she was eight feet, four inches tall as she stalked Denver.

Denver backed away slowly, conscious of Daylen's warnings since they were kids—never turn your back on a wolf.

She kept her eyes downcast and her throat exposed, because something was wrong with Tessa. Oh, she'd always been overbearing and aggressive, but it was more than that. She felt sick. She felt heavy. She stank up the air with the bitter scent of anguish. Tessa Hoda wasn't okay.

Denver cast a quick glance to the front window of Tessa's home, and the curtain dropped back down before she could see who was looking out at her—Stark, or Daylen.

"He's my friend," she said as her shoulder blades hit the side of her truck.

"You have no friends here, fox. If you are in

29

town and you see one of us, you will cross the street and stay out of our way. You won't talk to us. You won't message us. You won't even look at us, am I clear?"

"This isn't right." She'd said it as loud as she was able under the great weight of Tessa's dominance, and it came out a whisper.

"He doesn't want you here!" Tessa roared. "Do you understand?"

Another glance up at the window, and the curtain was perfectly still. Denver's eyes burned with sadness.

If he had wanted her here, he would've come out and stopped his mother.

Daylen had never been scared of Tessa. Tessa had always required respect through fear, and he wasn't afraid of anything, or anyone. It was why he'd always been the second son, despite being older than Vager.

"Yes. I understand."

Tessa hooked a finger under her chin and lifted her face. Denver's breath shook as she locked eyes with the she-wolf.

To her shock, Tessa's eyes were rimmed with tears. She'd never seen the Alpha cry in all the years she'd known her.

"There's no control. I need you to stay away."

Sick. Tessa was sick. Her wolf was sick, or...something.

Tessa opened Denver's door and stepped back as she got in. And that she-wolf stood there in the snow, watching her leave.

And Daylen really didn't come out to see her.

She'd held onto her belief that he was still her best friend for the last lonely couple of years, but she'd been wrong.

How did a loyal heart turn the devotion off? How did she tell the fox inside of her that he wasn't a friend anymore? How did she explain it when there was no reason? No closure?

Denver brushed her damp cheeks with the back of her hand quickly, because crying over someone who didn't care about her felt weak.

She'd been a stupid girl to hold on so long.

She wished Daylen had never come back at all.

FOUR

"How did that feel?" Stark asked from his seat at Tessa's dining room table.

Daylen clenched his jaw and watched Denver's truck disappear into the trees. Through the window, his mother turned and looked right at him.

With a sigh, he dropped the edge of the curtain and took his spot leaning against the wall. "It felt like nothing."

Stark lowered his newspaper from in front of his face and narrowed his eyes at Daylen. "The messed-up thing is you sound like you're actually telling the truth."

In a monotone, Daylen told him, "I have no reason to lie."

Stark set the newspaper onto the table and leaned his elbows against the wooden surface. "You guys were thick as thieves for years. You skipped out on Pack hunts to hang out with her, and now you can honestly say you feel nothing when your mother runs her out of the territory? Did you hear her sniffle? Right there at the end? Hmm?"

Daylen just stared at him. Stark wasn't going to get to him today.

"Only a demon would break a pretty little heart like that one," Stark said. "How did she look?"

Daylen shrugged up a shoulder and stared off into the kitchen. "Normal."

"Interesting. You'll tell the truth about feeling nothing when you see her, but you lie about what she looks like." Stark sneered. "Is she a dog now? Did she let herself go?"

Don't snap. Don't show him he's getting to you.
"What do you want, Stark?"

"A description. She was so fuckin' sexy when we left here. Maybe you didn't see it, because you grew up with her, but me? Oh, I noticed that hottie. Big soft tits bouncing around in those little tank tops she lives in during the summertime. Round ass made for big hands." Stark held up his hands. "Those sexy lips that are full and big and made for sucking di—"

"Stop it," Daylen demanded softly.

"Or what?" Stark stood and locked his arms on the table. "Stop it or what, Prince Hoda?"

Daylen swallowed hard. If this conversation didn't rile up his wolf, then the damn animal truly was broken.

Stark sneered. "I always wondered if you two fucked."

Daylen clenched and unclenched his fists. "She looks just the same, but sadder. Her hair is longer, still curly, and she's put highlights in it. Her nails are painted light pink, she's driving the same truck, and wearing that same hoodie she always wore."

"The big one?" Stark asked.

Daylen nodded once.

"The one from your high school?"

Fuck, he hated this dude. Why couldn't he have abandoned them with the rest of the wolves?

"Did you give that hoodie to her? Is she wearing it because it's yours? You fucked her."

Daylen shook his head. He was exhausted down to his very bones.

Truth be told, Denver looked very different, but not in any way he could explain to this asshole.

"I never fucked her," he said. "I never wanted to." And let him hear the truth in his tone now.

"Maybe I'll have a go at it, then," Stark said.

Daylen lurched forward and slammed his fists onto the table.

"There he is," Stark said through a baiting grin. "Big bad wolf, you've been hiding. It's been fucking boring around here without a little bloodshed."

"Boys, enough!" Tessa ordered from the doorway. "Marsden is here. We can start the meeting."

"You can throw that pretty little fox away all you want," Stark murmured. "I'll take good care of her."

Where the hell was his wolf? Where? Fury rippled through him, but he couldn't Change to save his life right now. Didn't hinder the rage that boiled through him though. Daylen flipped the table right onto Stark's lap. His chair shattered under him, and Daylen shoved the table backward, pinning Stark against the wall. Before he settled, Daylen slammed his fist against his face, and the crack of a jawbone breaking echoed through the room.

With a roar, Stark shoved the table, but Daylen was ready. He jumped over it easily and just as Stark was pushing upward, his fist cocked, gravity was pulling Daylen right to him.

"I said stop!" Tessa screamed, her tone saturated with rage and an Alpha's order.

Daylen's body went limp and he fell onto Stark, who had also lost control of his body.

Daylen pushed off him, and looked over to see Stark's eye color fade to almost white, and his face elongate. A snarl ripped out of him, but Tessa was crouched on the upended table, her own eyes blazing gold.

"Get. Out," she snarled to Stark. "Go Change in the woods and come back in here quiet. I can't handle Pack fights today. Surely you can understand I've been through enough." Her lips curled up over sharpening canines as she uttered to the both of them, "Give me a fuckin' break."

Chest heaving, Stark stood and made his way to the door. His legs were moving jerkily, like he was trying to fight Tessa's order. Over his shoulder he said, "Your mom always has to save you."

"Tessa doesn't have to protect me from shit, Stark."

"How sad," Stark yelled, "that you call your own mother by her first name."

And that's what Stark did. He dug at every scab in the Pack and never let up, never allowed things to heal.

The rage faded from Tessa's face, and she glanced at Daylen. "Vager should be here."

"Yeah? Don't I know it. If Vager was here, you wouldn't have to deal with me. You can say it. I wasn't the son you wanted to prep for this."

Tessa shook her head slowly. "No. You aren't the son I wanted for this." And that...that right there was why he called her Tessa, and not 'mom' or 'mother.' "Vager would've never brought a fox shifter into Pack territory," she sneered.

The benefit of numbness was that Tessa's venom didn't feel like anything today. Daylen stood and righted the table as Tessa eased back. He replaced the plastic vase that had fallen off and shoved the fake, dust-covered yellow flowers back into it. He set the chairs back where they went and offered Tessa an empty smile. "Gotta go. Busy day today."

As he made his way out of the house, Tessa's tired voice followed him. "We have a Pack meeting."

"Yeah? To talk about the future of this Pack?" He gestured to Marsden, who stood silently against the wall, his arms crossed and his eyes on the carpet. "You can have it with Marsden." He gestured outside. "And with Stark, when he's done with the Change that you forced on him. I have to go beg for my old job back and rebuild my life though."

"We should've never come back here," Tessa growled.

Daylen slapped his hand on the open doorframe and pointed to her. "Here is exactly where we were always going to end up. You know why? Because you ran us into the ground. And this?" He opened his arms to the house. "This is our fuckin' grave. We were happy here before you—"

"Happiness isn't part of our story—"

"We were as happy as we could be! You dragged every one of us away from our jobs, Tessa. Away from the territories that our wolves had claimed. Away from the safest place to Change and be ourselves, and then you forced us to live in that goddamn neighborhood and pretend to be human, and we aren't! We aren't good pretenders! You had us all tuck our wolves away and forget who we are, and for what?"

"Because he needed us."

"Because Vager needed us? He was in jail. He was only allowed visitors once a week. We could've made that trip every week, and still lived here. You wouldn't have hurt our wolves."

"I was grieving!"

"We all were!" he roared. "But you only saw your own pain. And when he went downhill, you focused on the girl, and you broke me over her."

Tessa narrowed her eyes. "That was your first duty as Second in this Pack. Vager would've wanted—"

"No. What I did?" Rage simmered right through him. Rage and guilt and regret. "What I did would've made Vager roll over in his grave. Twist things in your head however you want to, Tessa, but eventually, some night when you can't sleep, you're going to think about it. You weren't there, so I'll explain how it really was. Ruby. Was. Terrified."

Tessa yanked her gaze away from Daylen.

"I can still taste her blood—"

"Stop it—"

"I can still see the tears of pain streaming out of her eyes as she woke up with that goddamn bite on her arm."

"I said stop it!"

And he did. He had to. Tessa gave orders so easily, and he had to obey.

"Vager was good. He would've grown this Pack. He was devoted to me and what I wanted for all of you. He wanted to breed with a she-wolf of my choosing and continue the line, and what did you ever do, Daylen? You chased a fox your whole life and denied every suitable match, and skipped half the Pack meetings for nothing. You bought a house outside of Pack territory, and ignored every bit of advice I ever gave you. You always put this Pack second to your own needs. I wanted you to move to Montana with me and the rest of the Pack. I needed you away from that fox so you could get your head on straight and be a better wolf."

"Did it work?" he asked, already knowing the answer.

Tessa lifted her chin into the air and uttered her truth. "No. You're worse."

It should've hurt. This all should've hurt. He'd tried very hard for the entirety of his life to be the son Tessa wanted him to be, but he could never be Vager. Vager had been too perfect in her eyes and could never do anything wrong. He had been too much like Tessa, and she only understood wolves that were like her. "I did everything you ever asked, Tessa, even when the deeds you asked me to do were evil, so don't

43

preach to me about how Vager should be here. You're damn right he should be here. You had a moral compass when he was around."

He turned and left the house, but Tessa's words followed him out. "Even on his weakest days, Vager was stronger than you."

It should've been a blow, but it missed. Every insult missed right now. Vager was a ghost, and so was Daylen. Only difference was, Daylen was walking around here pretending to still be alive.

Daylen yanked the door of his truck open.

"Daylen!" Tessa called.

Daylen rolled his eyes closed and sighed. He twisted around. "What?" he asked the woman standing on her doorstep.

"Remember the order. Leave the fox alone."

He was tired. So tired. He felt like he'd aged ten years since he'd come back here. "Fine." He got into his truck and followed Denver's tracks down the driveway.

Fuckin' Tessa. She'd always felt so threatened by Denver, and he'd never figured out why. She'd been his friend, the one he'd leaned on and had fun with, the one who had allowed him to be himself, but Tessa had always given him shit for befriending a fox. Like they were beneath werewolves, but Daylen didn't see it that way.

Denver had been the most normal thing about his entire life.

She wasn't beneath anyone.

Likely Tessa had just needed to alienate him from anything that made him happy so he could be a good soldier, like Vager. Like Marsden. Like all the ones who left.

Not like Stark though.

Stark wasn't a good soldier for anyone.

The gray wolf stood in the middle of the snow-laden road, his blazing frost-blue eyes filled with hate. Daylen didn't slow down. If he ran over him, great. One less asshole in his life.

Stark slunk out of the way just in time to miss his tires, and he watched him leave. Daylen rolled down his window and stuck out his middle finger, retracting it just as Stark snapped with his teeth and tried to bite his hand off.

So predictable. Daylen rolled his window back up and turned the radio dial up to deafening, trying his best to drown out Tessa's damn order rattling around in his head.

Leave the fox alone. Leave the fox alone.

His inner wolf wasn't listening. He wasn't even awake, so Tessa's order didn't feel so heavy.

Ha. Now he really was the worst soldier.

FIVE

Stupid werewolf.

Stupid, stupid boy werewolf with his emotional constipation.

Denver hadn't done anything wrong, he was just mean!

And his rude mother! They didn't want her around? Fine. Fine!

But she had done a lot of work in stupid Daylen's house, and she was confiscating everything she'd bought for it.

Like these yellow curtains? Hers!

Denver removed the entire curtain rod and

marched it out to the burn pile she'd started. Now, a more frugal Denver would show up sometime tonight when her rage had dissipated, and she would mourn all the stuff she could've sold or added to the small home she'd stupidly purchased down the road, but enraged Denver didn't care about that stuff right now.

She tossed it onto the pile and marched back inside, pulled the two white chairs she'd found at a garage sale from the table, and dragged their legs through the snow before she hoisted them onto the burn pile.

She'd bought him cases of macaroni and cheese just because she knew he'd loved it, but she would be damned if he feasted on her presents! She yanked armloads of the boxes out of the pantry and muttered curses as some of them dropped onto the wooden floors on her way out. Whatever. Whatever!

She tossed those on the burn pile as well. The vase and dead flowers were next, along with the four sweatshirts she'd found for him at the general store, and the stupid file boxes she'd bought so he could organize his taxes and important papers. Then the picture collage of them she'd made on a pinboard made the pile too, because he shouldn't have access to any of the nice things she'd done for him!

She pulled a gas can from the back of her truck and emptied it, then tried to light a match, but failed because her hands were shaking with anger. It took three matches before the fire took and man, did the flames lick the sky.

Safe fire-burning tactics were out the window with a woman scorned, so she left it burning in the snow as she made her way inside and stomped her foot on the note she'd left, still floating around the floor in the breeze.

In a huff, she grabbed a pen from one of the kitchen drawers and scribbled a new note on the back of it.

Have a great life, worst friend.

She tried to draw a middle finger but it didn't look right. Whatever. What. Ever!

She went to replace the pen in the drawer, remembered she bought all those pens, and scooped up as many as she could, then carried them to the front door and flung them in the general direction of the burn pile. Her blankets and the dog bed by the door got thrown that way, too.

In a huff, she slammed the door and slapped the note onto it, took her third favorite pocket knife from her jeans, flicked it open, and stabbed that note into his door like a psychopath.

Today was going well, her mental stability was definitely intact.

She stomped over the snow, boots crunching as she snapped the pens, and she barreled out of his territory for the last time. Not even the fox would return here. It felt like there was an entire storm cloud inside her right now. The fox was just as hurt as the woman in her was.

Friends were supposed to be loyal—not drop

you like you were nothing.

Feeling utterly alone, Denver opened up a text to her sister, but the last thing Lyndi had written was, *Are you going to message Bartholomew?*

The question caught her off-guard. Bartholomew who? Wait, that was the fox shifter her parents were wanting her to pair up with.

Bartholomew, thirty-four, willing to relocate, something, something, something...

A pairing would mean she wouldn't ever be alone again. She and Bartholomew would be friends, like her parents were, and never leave each other, and make it work no matter what, because fox pairings were a very serious thing. Her fox could get attached to his, and she would never get hurt. He wouldn't be allowed to leave her. It would be safe.

She couldn't think straight. Her insides hurt from feeling betrayed and abandoned, and her head was swirling with confusing thoughts, and the fox was so sad.

Before she could change her mind, Denver opened her mother's photo of the prospects and memorized Bartholomew's information.

What could it hurt to make a new friend? She didn't have to pair up with him, but at the very least, she could have a buddy and not feel so damn lonely.

Yes. This was an awesome idea.

She entered his number into her phone, and typed out a message. It had like three typos, but if she stopped to edit them, she would change her mind so send, send, SEND!

Dear Bart. Can I call you Bart? Or do you prefer Bartholomew? My mame is Denver Mosley and my parents gave me your information. I'm a fox, like you, and just turned 30. And I cud use a friend. So if you could use a friend too, message me back. I like sushi, and sewing quilts, and I pay my own bills. Sincerety, Denver.

She was halfway down Daylen's winding

driveway when a response came through. Heart in her throat, she slammed on her brakes and skidded to a stop.

Dear Denver Mosley, I think you have the wrong number. My name is Craig, but yes you can call me Bart. I'm curious about this fox thing. Are you a furry? That's cool. I'm into whatever. I like ham sandwiches, sleeping under quilts, and anal. Sincerely, CraigBart.

"Oh my gosh," she muttered, checking the number. Yep! She'd texted the wrong number. Craig sounded weird.

In a rush, she copied her earlier message, sent this one to the right number, and then blocked CraigBart.

Denver blew out a steadying breath and set the phone in her cupholder, then gripped the wheel and began to drive again. Everything was going to be okay. Sure, it felt like she couldn't breathe and her heart was on fire, but she was still kicking and would just go say hi to Lyndi tonight and cope with the loss of her best friend in the safe and steady confines of her house, because a ridiculous amount of spicy chicken wings and a glass of cheap red wine were the solution to all things.

Today, she was going to let it hurt, but tomorrow?

She was going to start moving her life forward.

SIX

Your house is on fire.

Daylen narrowed his eyes at the text on his phone. Stark never gave up, did he?

His phone rang, and Stark's name came across the caller ID for the fourth time in a row.

"I'll see what we can do about the salary, but things are a little tighter around here since you left," Abel told him.

Daylen shoved his phone into his back pocket and stood to shake his former boss's hand. "Thank you for considering taking me back. I know I left you in a bind when I had to go."

Abel was an old lumberman with a thick silver beard and leather skin. His dark eyes were understanding when he said, "Some of the boys told me it was something to do with your brother. I imagine it was hard staying in a small town after something like that. We all heard about what he did. Bad bar fight, and your brother never had much of an off-switch. That seems like a mighty big shadow for you to escape."

He didn't know the half of it, and Daylen would rather step in a bear trap than explain any further, but he appreciated the understanding. "It'll all sort itself out," he murmured and then headed for the door.

"I'll talk to Terry and call you by three with the salary we can offer you. If it's too low, don't be worried about looking for something different. I would love to have you back here, but money is money. I'll still give you a reference if you decide on somewhere else."

Abel had always been a great boss to him. "I

sure appreciate everything. I'll have my phone's volume up for that call."

He tipped his head and made his way out of the office building on the west side of the sprawling lumberyard. A quick jog down the stairs and through a few mud puddles and he was to his truck. His phone had stopped vibrating at least. Maybe Stark had finally gotten bored of ruining his day.

He checked the time on his phone, and saw that there was a text with an image waiting. When he opened it up, it was a picture of the edge of the clearing near his home and smoke drifting up through the trees.

"Shit!" he snarled as he climbed into his truck. He was off like a shot the second he got his engine turned on.

He sped and skidded down every shortcut backroad to his house, and didn't slow until he reached the cabin.

What he saw in his yard dumbfounded him.

There was a scorching bonfire, the entire

clearing smelled like gasoline and smoke, and there was debris all over his yard.

It wasn't the house on fire...it was his furniture.

No...it was the pieces of furniture that had appeared before he'd come back. Denver's things.

He made his way around the fire and through the cluttered yard to the note on the front door.

Have a great life, worst friend.

It was in Denver's handwriting, but he didn't really understand why she'd drawn a cartoon dick at the bottom.

All right, the dick didn't make sense, but the words snapped against his heart like a rubber band. It stung a little, and besides rage and guilt, hurt was the first emotion he'd felt in days.

A soft growl rattled his throat as he read it again, and he froze.

There was the wolf. God, he'd thought he'd

lost the animal.

The wolf was probably angry at his territory being defiled.

Daylen pulled the knife from the door and shoved the letter in his pocket, then used the tip of the blade to push the door open slowly.

Now it looked like much more like it had when he'd left, except the floor was littered with macaroni boxes and writing pens. Weird.

She'd taken the bedding from the corner, too. That's probably what was piled in the yard near the bonfire.

This place smelled like her.

He inhaled deeply and the growl settled to nothing. A dozen memories assailed him with that smell. This was her specific scent when she was pissed off.

In the second grade, Ronald McCoy had called her a hairy squirrel and she'd gotten so mad, she'd punched him square in the throat. She'd smelled like this when she did it. When they were sixteen, Daylen had been driving too fast and crashed her car into a tree, and she'd smelled like this. He'd shut down on her when Vager was sentenced to a jail in Montana and she'd demanded he tell her everything, and when he'd refused...she had smelled like this.

Little fox could rage like a werewolf when she was riled up.

A little smile took the corner of his mouth, and Daylen pursed his lips to stop it. This wasn't funny. Okay, the little cartoon dick at the bottom of her angry note was a little funny.

She couldn't even rage without entertaining him.

Daylen made his way back to the bonfire and searched the contents of it, but most items had burned through and were unrecognizable. At the edge of the pile, though, there was a half-burned pinboard. Her face smiled back at him in a picture, and in a rush, he stooped and yanked the hot thing out of there.

His heart had turned to stone over the past two years, but staring at that smile etched a small crack in the rock he protected in his chest cavity.

He knelt and scooped snow onto the burning pictures. Most were completely gone, and the remaining ones were singed badly. He plucked the smiling picture of Denver from the metal flower pin that held it in place on the unfamiliar cork-board. Had she made this for him? For his home?

The picture was of Denver wearing a strapless dress, with dark lipstick on her full lips. She wore dark eyeliner under her moss-green eyes, and her dark curls were wild and full. Her eyes were half closed with a laugh, and he knew what the other half of the picture should look like, even though it was burned off completely. He had been there, holding her, carrying her over a mud pit. He remembered that dress, that smile, that shade of red on her lips, and that night.

She'd had a bad date, and the douche-bag had left her at the restaurant with no ride home. Daylen had gone to pick her up, and then he'd given her a fifteen-minute car ride out to the river, ripping her for her taste in men the whole ride, but knowing he was going to pay that asshole a visit later that night. She hadn't wanted to go home yet because her parents were so strict with her, and she'd been dating a human. She didn't want the I-told-you-so quite yet, so they'd gone to the river and sat on an old bench and drank cheap beer, and he'd made fun of her until she stopped crying and cracked a smile. She took this picture, a selfie, an hour later, when her high heels had stuck in the mud and he'd had to carry her to the truck like a damsel in distress. He'd dared her to run back and jump off the rope swing after this picture was taken, and she'd done it. Of course. Denver was always up for anything.

It's part of what made her so fun.

It's part of what had made her such a tempting escape.

He wished he'd been able to see the pictures she'd printed out before they had burned to ashes, because right about now, it felt so damn good to feel anything at all.

Leave the fox alone.

He just wanted to see something. Just wanted to test the waters a little bit.

He had Denver's number memorized, which he needed on his new phone. Tessa had smashed his damn last one.

Why did you draw a dick at the bottom of your note? Send.

He sat there in the snow and watched the fire burn for three full minutes before she responded.

It's a middle finger. She followed that explanation with a middle finger emoji and oooooh. He looked at the note again and yeah, he could see where she tried and failed to draw that.

What are you doing? Send.

Blocking you. Please leave me alone. You aren't the friend I thought you were.

It's a sin to burn macaroni and cheese. Send.

The message wouldn't go through though. He tried twice, and both times his phone told him it had failed to send.

Crap.

She'd never blocked him before.

All right, so...he'd been able to send her a text, which meant Tessa's order wasn't working like it was supposed to. Maybe the Alpha had lost her potency when his wolf got broken. He couldn't decide if ignoring an order was a good thing or bad thing.

The flashbacks came from nowhere. It always happened like this. He was in a moment that had nothing to do with Ruby Daughtry or what had happened over the last two years, but still, a memory of her laying on that damn barn floor whispering her mate's name mindlessly as she writhed in pain that Daylen had caused her exploded across his mind like a row of bombs going off.

"Stop," he whispered, closing his eyes tightly. But when he opened his eyes again, he was in the barn back in snowy Montana, pacing the dirt floor, hoping to God he hadn't killed her with his damn bite. Hoping she would survive. Hoping if she didn't, it would be fast either way.

Her wolf hated him. She wasn't the one he had chosen.

Gritting his teeth, Daylen uttered a curse and blinked hard again. The prickles of frost touched his cheeks, and when he looked up, it was snowing lightly. He'd never been so happy to see the storm clouds in the sky. They meant he wasn't in that barn—in that hell—anymore.

He laid back in the snow, rested his hands on his chest, and waited for his heart to stop racing.

It was good that Denver had blocked him.

More than she could ever understand, she'd been right.

He really wasn't the friend she'd thought he was.

SEVEN

Denver needed to practice her middle-finger drawing.

"Are you singing tonight?" Gary the Bartender asked. In her head she called him Gary the Bartender, because she'd never actually caught his real name and he didn't wear the name tag he was supposed to, so okay. If he was too cool for name tags, he had to deal with whatever she wanted to call him.

"Nah, not tonight. Tonight, I'm here for fun."

"I don't knowwww," he drawled out as he poured a mixed margarita into a glass of ice.

"You seem like you have fun on stage."

Fair enough. She actually did enjoy it. "I thought there was no live music on Thursday nights."

"Woman, there's an empty stage and a microphone, and a guitar that holds some tune. I've never seen you need much more than that."

"I'm just here saying hi to Lyndi. Is she in yet?"

"Yep, she's in the back doing inventory. We're having a hell of a time with supply issues. The trucks are coming in randomly and it's a crapshoot on what we get."

"Are you getting bottled soft drinks?" she asked innocently.

"You're the only one who comes to a bar and orders glass bottles of orange pop," he said, reaching into a miniature fridge under the counter. "I swear Lyndi only stocks these for you."

"It's the perk of having a sister managing a local bar."

"Mmm," he said, sliding the margarita to the lady at the end of the bar counter. "You could ask her to give me a raise if you want."

"Ha! Heck no, I'm not getting in the middle of that."

"Dang. Worth a shot. Lyndi!" he called to the back.

"Busy!" Came her sister's answer.

Gary the Bartender twitched his head toward the door behind the bar. "Your best shot at talking to her is going to be back near the freezer tonight."

Denver tipped an imaginary hat and strode behind the bar and down the hallway, past Lyndi's small office. She peeked her head around the corner of the storage room. "Hey."

"Oh my God, do you know how much drama you have caused today?" Lyndi asked, pulling her in for a fast, rough hug.

"What did I do?"

"You got in a fight with Mom and Dad, and messaged Bartholomew."

"What? How did you know?"

"Because he messaged our parents and told them you'd reached out."

"Well, that's unfortunate. He hasn't even responded to me yet," she grumbled.

"Did you go see Daylen?"

"Maybe."

"And?" Lyndi nearly shrieked the word and Denver shrugged her shoulders to her ears as they rang with the pitch of her sister's voice. Youch!

"And nothing," she mumbled. "He doesn't want to see me."

"Well, sometimes men have no idea what they are doing with their lives, and then they make stupid decisions, and then they lose all common sense, and then they lose track of literally anything a woman could want, and then—"

"Uuuuh are you okay?"

"Yes. I'm great." Lyndi pulled the pen from behind her ear and jotted down a number on her notepad, then started pushing bottles of Patron to the side to count them. "It's just sometimes men can be very dense, so maybe cut the wolf some slack."

Yep, she was in an alternate universe, clearly. "Cut the wolf some slack?" Denver repeated dumbly. "Since when have you grown a heart for Daylen? You hate him."

"No. No, no, no, I never said I hated him."

"You said on multiple occasions, and I quote, 'I hate that flea-ridden barbarian.'"

"Well...because he was annoying."

"Because he teased you, but you never figured out he was teasing and you got your feelings hurt all the time."

"Well, why did he have to tease all the time like that?"

"Because that's how wolves communicate."

"By insulting each other?"

"Yes. If they ignore you, then you should be worried. That would mean they're either hunting you, or you don't matter enough to pay attention to."

"You sure know a lot about wolf psychology."

"Probably more than the wolves. Sometimes they're dense, as you said."

Lyndi dropped her gaze. "Jake is pushing me away again." Aaaaah. That's where her man-speech had come from. "At least when Daylen was around, I never saw him push you away."

"Oh, you would be wrong about that. He pushed me away the day Vager got sentenced, and was distant for the entire year before he moved away. He never really came back." Denver had come here to vent about Daylen, but Lyndi seemed to be dealing with something bigger. She brushed her finger against Lyndi's arm, because foxes loved touch. "Jake will come around. You're still a pretty new pairing, and it's a lot. Sometimes boys need time and space."

Lyndi smiled and shook it off. "Of course. It'll all be fine. This is part of the ups and downs of being paired up. Our parents went through these phases a thousand times."

Hmm. Bartholomew's friendship seemed less appealing all of a sudden. She wanted steady coasting, not a roller coaster.

Men were a lot.

"How's work?" Lyndi asked.

"Aaah, the subject change. Smooth."

"Thank you, thank you, I've been working on my segues."

Denver sat on an empty crate. "Work's good, I'm up for a raise. I'm kicking butt and taking names."

"That's awesome." Lyndi wasn't really listening. She was counting bottles of bottom-shelf whiskey.

"I'm gonna let you get to it." Denver stood and made her way out. "Hey, Lyndi?"

Her sister turned, her dark eyebrows arched high in question. "Yeah?"

"Jake will come around." She used a twist on Lyndi's words when she said, "Cut the fox some slack."

"Don't choose Bartholomew unless he feels

important," Lyndi said in a rush.

Denver frowned. "I don't plan on choosing Bartholomew at all."

"It's just...the parents will have a plan and maneuver you into place. I guess what I'm saying is...don't get maneuvered into any place you don't want to be."

They'd never had a talk like this before. "Okay. I won't," she promised.

As she walked back down the hallway, Denver wondered what Lyndi was really trying to say to her. Had she been maneuvered by their parents in her pairing with Jake? She'd thought Lyndi had chosen him freely, but maybe there was more to it. Perhaps she hadn't been paying enough attention.

"You're getting song requests," Gary the Bartender said as she made her way past him.

"From who? There's about eight people in here and four are passed out already."

He locked his arms on the bar top and gave her the crooked smile that charming boys used to get girls to do what they wanted. He was flexing his triceps very hard. "I'm requesting a song. You owe me one for not talking to your sister about a raise."

Denver sighed. "What song?"

"Break It."

Well, now she was surprised. "You don't want a cover song?"

He began drying a glass with a dishcloth. "I like your originals best."

Huh. "One song, and then I'm blowing this popsicle stand. I have a big night planned." Chicken wing dinner, glass of red wine, romantic comedy, vanilla scented bath bomb, a good cry in the tub, in bed by nine, and then lie in the dark for three hours wondering what the hell had ever happened to that nice werewolf named Daylen.

"Two songs," he negotiated, "and I'll buy your next drink."

"You flirt with every woman who walks through that door, Gary. You probably have three girlfriends, and no idea what your type of woman even is. One thing is for certain though. It ain't me." She held up her orange soda. "I'm good with this one, thank you."

"My name isn't Gary. It's Tyler," he called after her.

"Same thing," she sang over her shoulder as she headed for the stage.

EIGHT

This was the test.

Daylen paused at seeing Denver's old Dodge parked over the line. She was truly terrible at parking.

Leave the fox alone.

He didn't really feel Tessa's order, just heard it in his head, repeated on a loop over and over. He reached out and brushed his fingertips across the scratch on the truck's door. He remembered when she'd gotten that. She scraped the truck down the side of a tree when they were out mudding five…no, maybe six years ago?

He'd offered to buff it out for her, but she said she liked the memory, so there that scratch remained.

Leave the fox alone.

Shut up, Tessa.

He shoved his hands deep into his pockets and sauntered across the cracked asphalt to the front door of Zaps Bar and Grill.

This was another test, because Denver would be in there. *Woooolf, better stop meeee.*

The wolf remained silent.

Daylen pulled the door open and did a quick scan of the room.

There she was, talking to the bartender.

Not wanting to be seen just yet, he sidestepped into the dark front corner and took a seat on the little bench there.

Denver had changed out of his old hoodie and was wearing tight black jeans, scuffed leather booties, and a tight, long-sleeved shirt in a forest-green color that he knew would match her eyes, if he could see them. Her dark, curly hair really was longer, almost down to her shoulder blades now. She'd put some caramel-colored streaks in it. It was different, but he liked it. He would never tell her that. He would tell her she looked weird just to get the eye-roll from her. It had been their way, before everything went to shit.

The bartender leaned on the bar, and the wolf perked up. His eyes were hungry, and his smile flirty, and Daylen leaned his elbows on his knees and strained his hearing. The jukebox was loud, but he could make out their conversation.

"I'm requesting a song," he told her. "You owe me one for not talking to your sister about a raise."

Ha. Good luck, bub. Denver didn't sing in front of strangers. She'd had stage fright since she was a fetus.

Denver let off this little laugh that Daylen didn't like, but he didn't know why. She sighed. "What song?"

The bartender's answer was immediate. "Break It."

"You don't want a cover song?" she asked him.

He began drying a glass with a dishcloth. "I like your originals best."

What the actual fuckery was this? Denver didn't sing. Not in front of anyone but Daylen and Lyndi.

"One song, and then I'm blowing this popsicle stand. I have a big night planned."

"Two songs," he negotiated, "and I'll buy your next drink."

The wolf rattled a soft growl in Daylen's chest, and he leaned back and canted his head. Maybe she was dating the bartender.

"You flirt with every woman who walks through that door, Gary," Denver said. "You probably have three girlfriends, and no idea what your type of woman even is. One thing is for certain though. It ain't me." She held up her orange soda. "I'm good with this one, thank you."

"My name isn't Gary," the bartender called out as she walked toward the small stage in the corner. "It's Tyler."

"Same thing," she answered.

Daylen snorted. There she was. *Sorry, bartender, Denver is way too much woman for you.* Daylen knew that much from the bonfire litter all over his front yard. He didn't like the bartender. But why? He hadn't done anything wrong, and Denver had turned him down cold.

A group of six came in the front doors, and the accompanying gust of wind rattled his thoughts loose. He scooted to the far end of the bench, as far into the shadows as he could, and pulled his baseball cap lower over his eyes.

Denver climbed the stairs without a hitch in her step, and without hesitation, she picked up an acoustic guitar that was on a stand by a drum set. She dragged a three-legged stool over to the microphone and sat on it comfortably.

Wait. Wait.

Daylen looked around at the people starting to pay attention to her. One of them whistled, and Denver smiled. Oh, she blushed bright pink in the cheeks, but she didn't run off the stage.

She plucked a few strings and adjusted the tune, and then she clicked the microphone on. "Test, one, two. Can you hear me back in the back?"

For a split second he thought she meant him, but she was looking at the rowdy six-top that were settling into their seats at the big table in the middle of the room. She winced slightly under the light the bartender turned on, just over where she sat on the stage.

"There it is. Gary over there requested a song called Break It, but I've had a long day, and tonight I'm feeling a different one. Forgive me, Gary," she said with a grin and an apologetic duck of her head.

The first picked notes of a song rang out, and Denver hummed a pretty sound.

Mesmerized, Daylen leaned forward and rested his elbows on his knees again, clenched his fists in front of his mouth and relaxed into a song he never would've called in a million years.

Denver was different.

Over the past two years, she'd grown into something he didn't recognize.

I wouldn't have called it

Wouldn't have called you, but I know it's what we gotta go through

Here and gone and now all that's left is me and this microphone

Where did I go? Did you take me too?

Always thought it would be me and you

I'm still here and now I know

You had to run away, you had to let go

Cause the only thing that's real around here anymore

Is the way I feel, the way you don't

And nobody really has it in them to say no

It's easier to pack up and go

Do it fast, don't do it slow, boy

Fuuuuuuck.

Chills rippled up his arms. He'd always

known she had a voice, but this was something else. This was a woman on fire. A woman who had figured herself out.

She had her eyes closed and was playing her heart out, belting out every note. Magic was happening in here, and he was the dumbass who had never realized Denver had it in her.

She hit the chorus again, but this one was deeper, and when a tear fell out of the corner of her eye, he wanted to disappear.

He'd wished he could feel again, and now he would do anything to go back to the way he was.

She was hurt.

He'd hurt her.

He could hear it in the heartbreak of those lyrics.

Daylen felt watched, and when he looked over at the bar, Denver's sister Lyndi was leaned up against the bar top, eyes on him. She offered him this little sad smile, and then dragged her attention back to Denver. Beside Lyndi, the bartender was falling in love with Denver. He could see it in his eyes. He'd stopped in the middle of mixing a drink and was just watching Denver with an intensity that made Daylen want to rip his throat out for reasons he didn't understand.

His damn wolf was so broken.

The song was almost done. She was picking the guitar slower, and her vocals were relaxing. She opened her eyes and smiled at the six-top, who were already clapping and cheering.

Pretty smile. Okay, she'd always had a pretty smile. An easy one with perfectly straight, white teeth, and she shined her full lips with that pink lip-shit girls always used to attract idiots like Gary or Tyler or whatever the hell his dumb name was.

Tessa's order wasn't working. He wasn't on fire being this close to Denver. Even Tessa's voice had faded from his head, and now all he heard was Denver's songbird voice.

She commanded the entire room, and she did it easily, with no nerves. She was comfortable up there.

Never in a hundred years would he have imagined her doing this.

He'd shrank while he was away, but Denver? She'd grown into her own skin. Good for her. But a part of him regretted not being there to watch the change. He'd missed a damn good show.

Tessa had been right. They should've never come back here.

One day in and he was already testing orders and wishing to go back to a life that didn't belong to him anymore.

She was good.

Denver was good.

Better even, perhaps.

He nodded to himself and stood to leave.

Denver was turning off her microphone as she chewed on the corner of her lip, and her eyes locked right on him. There wasn't a hint of surprise there. Clever fox had known he was here. She gave him a smile that looked a lot like Lyndi's sad one. Her eyes were such a crystalline goldish-green under that saturated stage lighting.

He'd always known his friend was a stunner. She'd turned heads everywhere they went. Stark had asked if she'd let herself go, but no. She was even prettier now.

Everything was different.

He stood there, frozen in her gaze for a three-count before he forced himself to tip his baseball cap and walk out that door.

It was enough.

Seeing her like this was enough.

She was all right.

NINE

Daylen was leaving. That was him, right?

He wore an Atlanta Braves baseball hat low over sunglasses. Despite the snowy weather outside, he only wore a thin, white, long-sleeved shirt, which meant she couldn't see any of his tattoos to make certain it was him.

He was the same height as the Daylen she remembered, but this version of him had packed on muscle in the time he'd been gone. His shoulders and biceps pushed out against the thin cotton of his shirt, and his waist tapered into a V. She could practically see his abs from here, and in that dark corner, the lighting wasn't even all that great.

She was disappointed. That was the word—disappointed. She'd expected so much more from him and he'd let her down.

He was still letting her down by leaving without saying a word. It wasn't fair.

She settled the guitar on the stand and hopped off the stage. The big table stopped her on the way out, but she only spent a few seconds with them before she excused herself.

He would be long gone by the time she made it to the parking lot.

The salt and sand mixture that had been laid out on the icy parking lot crunched against the rubber soles of her dressiest booties. She didn't even know why she'd come here. This place was usually dead until ten or eleven o'clock, but she'd wanted to be around people, and see Lyndi, and feel like the world still existed.

She scanned the parking lot for his truck, but he wasn't at it. Instead, he was standing in front of her Dodge, leaning on the grill, looking down at the snow so his face was completely covered by the brim of his hat.

"Is it you?" she asked, approaching slowly.

He removed his sunglasses and hooked them on the neck of his shirt, then dragged those gold eyes up to her. He never was good at controlling his eye color, like she was. His wolf was too big. Or at least she thought he was. Denver sniffed the air, but he just smelled like cologne and man, and just a teeny, tiny hint of fur. He used to be straight wolf. Huh. He had a long scar from his hairline down through his left eyebrow and to his cheek. That was new. Werewolves healed fast, so whatever had done that to his face must've been a hard injury to recover from.

Denver stopped a couple yards shy of him. "Why? Why did you leave?"

He shrugged one shoulder up and shook his head. "I'm not going to have the answers you want."

"Forty-seven."

He frowned. "Forty-seven what?"

"Forty-seven is the number of texts I sent you that went unanswered."

Daylen ran his hands down his jaw. "My phone broke."

"Did you break it?"

He shook his head.

"Why didn't you get a new one?"

"I did, just with a different number."

"Why?"

He huffed a frozen breath and straightened his spine, looked longingly toward his truck.

Denver closed the distance between them and shoved him in the shoulder. "Why?"

He shook his head again, denying answers she so desperately needed.

"Why?" she asked louder, shoving him again. "Why, why, why, why did you leave me like that, to feel like I did something unforgiveable? Why did you leave me here to deal with my life alone? Why did you shut me out? Why did you break your phone, the only connection to me, and decide a new number would be best? Huh? So I couldn't contact you?"

"No, that's not...it's not..."

She shoved him again, harder. "Why, Daylen! After all we went through, you owe me closure. You owe me an explanation. The very least you can do is put me out of my fuckin' misery and explain to me that, 'no, Denver. It isn't your fault I abandoned you,' because that's what you did! You abandoned me, and this whole fuckin' time it felt like I did something so wrong to make you leave like that, only for the life of me, I can't recall what I did to make you hate me."

She went to hit him, but she got one fist against his chest before he wrapped her up tight and pinned her arms at her side. "You aren't doing that. We've never hurt each other."

"You hurt me!" she sobbed. She struggled, but it was futile. Daylen had always been ten times stronger than her. Her legs buckled and he held her upright and rested his cheek against the top of her head.

"I didn't break the phone. Someone broke it for me. I was ordered to leave without saying a word to anyone because we were going through something bad. The Pack was suffering. It's not how it used to be, Denver. I'm Second now."

"Vager's Second—"

"Vager's dead," he uttered in the softest snarl she'd ever heard rattle from his chest.

She gasped. Vager was dead? Daylen's younger brother was dead? But...no. He'd gone to jail for killing a man, and he was serving his sentence.

"Hanged himself." She'd never heard pain like that infiltrate two words more.

Breath hitching, she clapped her arms around him and held on as tight as she could, gripping the back of his shirt in her fists. Daylen loved Vager very, very much.

God, this hug felt important.

"I'm not supposed to be here," he told her.

"Why not?"

"Because my Alpha ordered me to leave the

fox alone." He released her suddenly and she stumbled backward. His gold eyes looked tortured. "The last two years, my life has revolved around orders. Do you understand?"

But...why? Why was he ordered to cut ties with her? "What did I do wrong?" she asked.

Daylen put his sunglasses back on, used them like a shield so she could no longer see the emotions on his face. "Nothing, Denver. You did nothing wrong. You just put too many forks in my road, and I have responsibilities I have to fulfill now."

Stupid tears. Stupid tears, stupid crying, and stupid emotions. Denver wiped her knuckles underneath her leaking eyes, and nodded. "That's going to be a really lonely and narrow path, Daylen, but okay. I'm not going to beg for friendship. I'm worth more than that. I'm a great friend," she gritted out. "And no matter what they make you feel or think, you were a great friend to me, too."

"I'm not. You don't understand what I have

done."

"What *is* it?" she asked. "What's so awful that you can't tell me? It's me, Daylen! It's always been me. Nothing can be that bad because I know you. What is it?"

He denied her again, just shook his head. Shook his head. God, she hated when he did that.

She huffed a humorless laugh. "This feels familiar—the shutdown. Tell Tessa she doesn't have to worry about a little fox in the wolf den. I'm getting paired up. You can make your own forks in your road."

He'd been looking at the snowy ground, but his head snapped up. "What do you mean?"

"It's fox stuff, Daylen. I have responsibilities, too."

She could feel him watching her, feel his attention on her as she got into her truck, but she didn't look at him. Just backed out of her parking space and headed out of the parking lot, away from him.

She supposed he had tried to give her some

closure. He'd said she didn't do anything wrong, and she was going to have to hold onto that as she moved forward with her life.

Chicken wings, red wine, bath bomb, good cry in the tub, bed, stay awake thinking about the friend Daylen used to be.

That conversation hadn't changed her plans for the night—not even a little.

At a red light a couple blocks down, her phone screen lit up with a text. Heart in her throat, she pulled it from the cupholder and read the message. Her disappointment was infinite when she figured out the unknown number wasn't Daylen's. It was Bartholomew.

Hello foxy lady. I feel like I can say that because your parents sent me pictures of you. Nicely done, genetics, lol. Sorry it took so long to get back to you. I wanted to make sure it was a good situation before I contacted you back. In the interest of honesty, I've been contacted by three other potential mates, and am also talking to them. Your parents assured me you are single with no prospects, so it will streamline things a bit for me. I would love to have a phone conversation if you are still up for talking. What time would you like me to call?

A car honked behind her. Oh crap, the light had turned green. Denver dropped the phone back in the cupholder, gripped the steering wheel, and hit the gas.

Bart had four prospects total, and was open about talking to all of them. That was good, right? At least he was honest? And she had no claim on his exclusiveness, because they didn't know each other. But she definitely didn't like that he'd talked to her parents to make sure she didn't have prospects. So, he could talk to other foxes, but she couldn't? Grody. And what pictures had her parents sent him? She felt exposed.

She needed to think on all of this before she responded with, *Good luck with the others.*

Today had been the most confusing day of

her entire life.

TEN

Tessa had smashed his damn phone two years ago, so he'd lost all the selfies and pics he had with Denver, and now all Daylen had to reminisce with was the half-burned picture of her laughing.

She was right. She'd been a great friend to him. Even now, when she had no reason to speak to him, she'd still asked for answers and hugged him when she'd found out about Vager.

It had felt so damn good to be held like that. Better than anything he could remember. Wolves liked touch, but this Pack didn't value touch anymore. They hadn't since Tessa had moved them to Montana.

Everything had gotten so broken.

The old wooden bed creaked as he relaxed his arms onto his knees and leaned his weight forward. The singed picture dangled between his fingers as he stared at the wall. Denver had always been his safe spot, and until tonight, until he saw her again, he hadn't realized how good it felt to be around her. He'd always taken that part for granted. Denver had always just been there, ever since he could remember, and she was light and fun and happy no matter what shit-show he was going through. Being away from her for the last couple of years had been hard, but seeing her again tonight? That had been eye-opening.

Denver made things better.

Pairing up? Good for her. Right?

He looked at her picture again and hated the emptiness that swallowed his insides up.

Pretty Denver would make some fox very happy. How could she not? She was light and happy and funny and obviously beautiful. The damn bartender could barely take his eyes off her tonight and Daylen understood. Hell, they were just friends, and he'd seen her through all of her awkward years, but even Daylen had had trouble taking his attention off her.

Damn, her voice matched her face. Stunner. And that confidence? How many times had he told her confidence was the most attractive thing about the girls he'd dated, and sometime in the last two years, when he wasn't paying attention, she had evolved and now she outshined everyone in this town.

That hug...

His shirt was still wrinkled in the back from where she'd grabbed him. His stomach had gotten queasy when he'd backed out of that embrace.

And when she'd shoved him...the devil in him had awoken and wanted to do something awful. Her feeling enough to push him like that was hot, those soft green eyes engulfing in flames, her little canines sharpening as she lit him up. A monstrous side of him had wanted to grab her by the back of the neck and drag her into him, pin her against the truck, and kiss her until she stopped yelling at him. He wanted to steal the words from her, taste them, get lost for just a few seconds and pay the consequences later.

He was so damn broken.

The front door opened and Daylen jumped up like a shot. He rushed to the living room to find Stark stomping snow off his boots. He had a duffle bag slung over his shoulder and was chomping on gum. Stark's eyes drifted to Daylen's hand.

"What are you going to do with a knife that you can't do with the wolf?" he asked.

Baffled, Daylen looked down at the long buck knife he held. He didn't even remember picking it up.

"What are you doing here?" he asked.

"Moving in," Stark said simply as he lifted the recliner that must've gotten flipped in Denver's earlier tirade. He sank into it and linked his hands behind his head.

"The fuck you are," Daylen said. He pointed to the door. "Get out!"

"No can do. At least not tonight. I got my old job back, but my old apartment complex is completely full until March."

"Then go wolf and sleep in the woods. You aren't staying here."

"Tessa says otherwise. She's given me babysitting duties. It's just me and you, roommate."

"You mean you tried to move in with Tessa and she told you to fuck off?" Daylen asked.

"Pretty much. Want to go halfsies on cable?" Stark asked, clicking around on the remote.

Daylen lost his shit and threw the knife. It sank deep into the cushion about an inch away from Stark's ear.

Stark blinked slowly and his eyes blazed almost white as he glared at Daylen. "You missed."

"On purpose. That's the last miss you'll ever get from me. Go figure your shit out somewhere else. I'm not rooming with the person I hate the fuckin' most." Daylen opened the door and snarled, "Get. Out."

Jerkily, Stark stood and stumbled toward the door. "No. No, no, no! Crap. Daylen, stop!"

Daylen laughed, watching Stark's dumbass get sucked out the door like he was possessed by a ghost who had took control of his body. This was awesome. "You have to obey my orders now, don't you?"

"Give me my bag!" Stark yelled as he fell on his tailbone in the front yard.

Daylen chucked it at his face so hard, Stark barely caught it in time.

Stark peeled his lips back over sharpening teeth and roared an enraged sound, but Daylen just gave a two-fingered wave and slammed his door.

No way in the world was he sharing his home with Stark, of all people.

He would rather be locked in a room with a rabid honey badger.

He would rather drink expired beer for the rest of his life.

He would rather take buckshot to his left butt cheek.

He would rather be a vegan werewolf.

Stark could move into his house when ferrets learned to knit socks.

He turned to his home and scanned the mess he hadn't yet cleaned from Denver's tirade. He caught a glimpse of himself in the front window and allowed a three-second stare down with the stranger in the reflection. That damn scar. Oh, he'd deserved it. Deserved the curse of the reminder. Every time he looked in the mirror now, he flashed back to the monstrous thing he'd done. It was a good punishment, never being able to move on, never being able to forget the type of man he was. It was fair.

Head loud with the memories of how messed up he'd been not-so-long ago, he began to clean.

He would have the lights turned back on tomorrow, but wouldn't be able to get the water switched back on for a couple of days. He would have to go pay the overdue bill and hope they could turn it back on sooner rather than later.

He'd accepted the salary his boss had texted him and would start work on Monday. He was back in his den, back to working on the home, and everything should feel like normal, but it didn't. Everything felt different because *he* was different now.

His old life felt like a lifetime ago.

Living room cleaned and swept, Daylen opened the front door to set the bags of trash outside.

Stark was still here. He was in his Camaro, his elbow on the window, his head resting in his hand. He didn't even look up as he pressed his middle finger against the window.

Daylen wished the wolf would come out so he could eat that dumb motherfucker. He hated him in his territory, but showing Stark that he bothered him would only get him picking at Daylen more.

He was obnoxious.

Shaking his head, Daylen went back inside and shut the door. He hooked his hands on his hips and looked around. Oh, this place needed a lot of work, but it looked a helluva lot better than it had earlier.

Daylen made his way to the single bedroom, plugged his phone into the wall charger, and set it on the nightstand before he remembered he didn't have any damn power yet. He didn't recognize the night stand. Denver must've forgotten to throw this one out. He hadn't bought it, but it looked like a nice, sturdy, worn piece. Denver probably got it at a garage sale or something. He liked it.

He opened the drawer and put his knife inside it, then set the picture of Denver by his phone.

Pretty woman. He was proud of her for how far she'd come.

She was going to make a really good mate for someone. Why did that blade of jealousy slash through his insides? She deserved to pair up. Pairing up was an honor in the fox community.

That dude better never break her heart though, or Daylen would eat his.

Just to test, he typed her number into his phone, and saved her contact. Tessa's order wasn't even rattling around his head anymore. Maybe her wolf was broken, too. Maybe she'd broken the entire Pack.

Why was there a dog bed by my front door? Delete, delete, delete.

Huffing a sigh, Daylen laid back on his bed and stared at the stationary ceiling fan. God, she was a fun distraction from the mess in his head.

Maybe she'd gotten a dog but she was respecting the wolf den, so she made it sleep outside. She'd always wanted one of those little basset hound puppies, but the critters cost an arm and a leg.

Messaging her would open up a lid to a chest

of memories and temptation that he couldn't close again, and for the life of him, he couldn't figure out if that was fair to Denver.

What did her boyfriend look like? She'd dated a few guys but they never stuck. And they always, always had a problem with his and Denver's friendship. Signs of insecurity. She needed a strong man. One completely secure in himself who would take the time to understand her.

Basset hounds were pretty cute.

Why was there a dog bed by my front door? Send.

Fuck. He threw the phone on the bed face-up and paced the room for a full five minutes. Time after time, his eyes went back to the phone screen, but she wasn't responding. He hoped she unblocked him soon.

He understood. He'd hurt her badly and it was stupid of him to think he could just text her a random question after two years of ignoring her and she would jump at the chance to talk to him.

Denver was different now.

He should make some macaroni and cheese. Crap, his water wasn't turned on, so there was no way to boil the pasta. He strode into the kitchen and pulled the fridge door open just to see. There was nothing in there. Huh. She must've cleaned it all out so it didn't rot when his power got shut off.

She really was something.

His phone rang in the other room, and Daylen froze. Was he imagining it?

Another ring, and he bolted into the bedroom and fumbled to pick up the phone. He cleared his throat. "Yeah?" he answered coolly.

"What are you doing?" Denver asked.

"Trying to make mac and cheese, but—"

"Not physically, Daylen. I mean why are you texting me in the middle of the night after you've made it pretty damn clear I'm not allowed in your life?"

Oh. That. Daylen straightened up and hooked

a hand on his waist, searched his room for inspiration. "I'm just...bored."

"I'm hanging up—"

"Wait! You didn't answer my question. Did you get a puppy?"

A tired sigh came through the phone. "No. The puppy I want would cost me a month of my mortgage."

"Mortgage? Did you move out of your apartment?"

"Yes. I moved eight months ago."

"Soooo, you have a house now?"

"I do," she said shortly.

"That's...congratulations. You've wanted to get out of your apartment for a long time."

"Yeah, I have to work early in the morning."

"Right. Yeah, right." He rubbed his eyes and wished he was doing better at this. "Your boyfriend. Is he nice to you?" The words fell out of his dumbass mouth before he could stop them.

Denver was quiet. Silent, in fact. He couldn't even hear her breathing.

"Hello?" he asked, thinking she'd hung up on him.

"It's an arranged pairing," she said softly. "I haven't even met him yet, and he's choosing between me and a few other prospects."

"The fuck?" he snapped. "So, you're what? Competing with other girls? Foxes? Fox girls? For some douche-ball's attention?"

"Goodnight, Daylen."

"Wait!" He scrubbed his hand down his three-day scruff. "The dog bed."

Another three-count of silence met him, and then, as soft as a breath, she admitted, "My fox kept going to your place. I put a bed out there for her, and that was her spot. She missed you very much."

His heart was drumming ridiculously heard against his ribs right now. "And you? Did you miss me?"

"You know the answer to that, Daylen. I wasn't the problem. You were."

Sometimes girls needed to hear the secrets

that men coveted. They needed to hear that they meant something. "I missed you, too," he said gruffly. "It was a really long couple of years without you." The line went silent again, and Daylen waited. "Denver?" he asked. There was this little sniffle that ripped at his guts.

"Yeah?" she asked in a thick voice.

"Everything is going to be all right."

"For me or for you?" she asked softly.

"For you," he promised.

"That's the thing, Daylen. To me, you were always the important one. It's hard to switch that off when it's your whole life."

He wanted to say the same sentiment back to her, because it was the truth. Because she'd always been special, had always been an incredible friend, had always been there, and loyalty like that was nearly impossible to come by in this world.

She gave all of herself unconditionally, and never kept tabs, never asked for repayment.

And that...that's why he'd chosen for all those

years to pay attention to her over Pack business.

But telling her that now, when she was so raw and he was so fucked up from what he'd done, wasn't fair. It was too much, too deep, too fast.

"Stark is camping in my front yard," he said, trying to lighten the subject and stop her tears.

She giggled thickly. "He's a pill."

"He's decided he's going to live here, so I'm probably going to kill him tomorrow."

"Oh," she said lightly. "Well, invite me to the funeral. I'll bring the shrimp cocktail."

Daylen made a gagging sound. "You bring that seafood shit around here and I'll never forgive you."

Now her laugh was downright gleeful. She'd only brought that up because she knew he hated shrimp.

"Where did you get the scar on your face?" she asked.

Mayday. Retreat. "From a fight I'm not ready to talk about."

"It's kinda hot."

Wait...what? "Umm, you wouldn't think that if you knew where I got it. Tell me about the new house. Paint a picture for me."

There was a smile in her voice when she said, "Once upon a time, I bought an almost microscopic two-bedroom, one bathroom house on five acres."

"Oooh," he said, impressed. "The fox went and got her some territory."

"Yeah, and it backs up to national forest that can't be settled."

Daylen frowned and sat up. "Wait, like my house?" The whole reason he'd bought this dumb house was because it was on twenty acres and backed up to forest that would never be built upon.

"Admission, I bought the old Cramer house."

Utterly shocked, Daylen asked, "Next door to my property?"

"Yup. Pretty sad, huh? I'd been shopping before you left, and they kept dropping the price.

And then my realtor told me to make an offer and they would consider it, so I scooped this place up."

Daylen padded out of his bedroom and to the big picture window on the west side of the house. Straight through those snowy woods, Denver was on the phone talking to him right now. She was so close.

It settled something ugly in him. Something that had been eating a hole in his chest.

He didn't feel so lonely.

And then there was a shift in focus to his damn reflection, to the scar Denver thought was hot, but was really part of the reason his wolf was dead.

He backed away from the window. "It was crazy seeing you sing tonight," he murmured.

"Yeah. I got over the stage fright, I guess."

"When did it happen?"

"About a month after you left. I didn't feel much back then. It's less scary to get in front of people when you don't care about anything."

He understood that down to his bones. He recognized her description of the numbness that now consumed him...whenever he wasn't talking to Denver.

"How's the Pack?" she asked.

"All gone. The Sheridan Pack barely exists anymore."

"I saw all the for-sale signs in their yards today. You werewolves are crazy."

"Don't I fuckin' know it. I'm stuck with Tessa, Stark and Marsden now. That's the Pack I'm inheriting."

"Nah. You aren't inheriting a Pack unless you want the scraps. You are Daylen Hoda. You survived being the second son, were built in violence, and your wolf is a monster. You can create whatever Pack you want. You don't need Tessa's legacy. You can make your own."

"And that, Denver, is why Tessa thinks you put too many forks in my road. Dangerous little fox."

"Clever little fox," she corrected him.

"Hey remember that one time you burned half my shit on my front lawn and then gave me life advice in the same day?"

Her laugh was like coming home exhausted to familiar sheets. The clear, genuine tone of it enveloped him and warmed his insides.

"I barely remember. It was so long ago."

"I start work back at the lumber yard on Monday," he said.

"Wow. Abel is letting the riffraff back in, huh?"

"My lunch breaks will still be the same."

She grew quiet. "What are you asking?"

This was stupid, and too fast. There had been a canyon between them and he didn't have any right to push them back to the way it was. She deserved time before he asked her for favors.

"Oh, nothing. Forget I mentioned it. I know you have work tomorrow, so I should let you go."

"Okay," she murmured.

"Denver?" he asked before she could hang up.

"Yes?"

He swallowed hard. "I'm sorry."

She exhaled a shaking breath. "For what?"

Daylen lifted his eyes to the mirror resting against the wall. That damn scar, and those damn wolf eyes that wouldn't go away. The wolf had been hurt, and now the monster was frozen inside of him.

His fault.

"I'm sorry for everything."

ELEVEN

This was probably a horrible idea.

Denver pulled to a stop next to a tent in Daylen's side yard and frowned at the giant who sat in a bag chair sipping a steaming cup of coffee next to a campfire. Stark had cut his blond hair into a mohawk and had it pulled back into a top knot. It was way better than the messy hair he used to hide his face with.

He was wearing a pair of jeans and nothing else.

"Aren't you cold?" she asked as she got out.

His eyes crinkled at the corners with his

smile. "If you've come to see Daylen, he already left for work."

Crud. "He works the early shift now?"

"Yup. He leaves at four thirty in the morning. Gotta get here before dawn to get that Daylen dick."

"Oh my gosh, now I remember how annoying you are. Why are you camping in his yard?"

"Because we are a Pack, and Pack members like to live together in harmony."

"So, you're homeless?"

The smile faded from his face. "Temporarily. Are you renting any rooms at your place, Sex Kitten?"

"Ha! To you? No thanks, never."

"You're fucking with his head," Stark called out as she moved to leave.

Denver peeked back around the front of her truck, taking the bait. "What do you mean?"

"Would you like some coffee?" Stark asked, lifting a blond brow high. He kind of looked like one of those Vikings on that television show she'd binge-watched last year.

"I had two cups before I drove over here. Liquid courage, and all."

"Mmm. You know Tessa found out he went to see you at that bar the other night."

"Yeah?" she asked in a dead voice. "How did she find out?"

"I told her."

Rat. "Why are you here, Stark?"

"To watch over our future Alpha, and make sure he stays on the straight-and-narrow."

"And what does the straight-and-narrow look like?"

"He's being trained by Tessa. She has to make up for a lot of lost time because she put all her eggs into one basket, and Daylen wasn't holding that basket."

"I don't know what that means."

"Yes, you do. You're a smart woman, Denver. Too smart for your own good, perhaps."

She huffed a frozen breath and made her way to Stark, grabbed the other empty fold-out chair and wiped the snow off the seat, then took it across the campfire from him. She slapped the legs down into the snow and took a seat. "Getting into a conversation with you never got me anywhere."

"Maybe I've changed," Stark said through a goading smile.

"I highly doubt it."

"Momma Wolf had two pups. One was cut out for Alpha from birth, and one was too quiet, cared too little, didn't want to form bonds, didn't want to maintain them, and the politics were lost on him. So Momma Wolf, being the good Alpha she was, put her focus into the viable son."

"The viable son," Denver repeated in a murmur. Her stomach turned.

"I didn't make these rules up," Stark said. "I wasn't even around when most of them were made. My bond, as you remember, is only five years old with this Pack."

"And you made every day hard, from what I also remember."

His smile reached his eyes this time. "Thank you. When Momma Wolf lost the viable son, she was forced to look at the second son for the first time. She has a big job. Guide him, mold him, train him in all the ways she did her first son. Only now he's older and set in his ways, and you know the saying about how you can't teach an old dog new tricks."

Denver swallowed down a growl. "How about Momma Wolf doesn't teach him any tricks, because he's already better than her."

Now Stark's smile filled with wickedness. "And that, little fox, is why the big bad Momma Wolf is going to kill you someday. Which she told Daylen yesterday. He won't be talking to you anymore. It's for your own protection. You get in the way of his destiny. You understand destiny, don't you? Like you and Bartholomew Hanson. Or should I call him Bartholomew Handsome? He's a looker, that one. You make a good-looking pair."

Her heart stuttered a beat. "How do you

know about him? Did Daylen tell you?"

"Fuck no. The only thing Daylen's said to me in the last two days is 'I hope you fuckin' freeze to death out here,' and he gave me this black eye." He pointed to his right eye, but all that was left was a slight green bruising around the outside. Fast healer.

"You probably deserved it."

"Oh, absolutely. He's not as much fun anymore though. Can't Change into the wolf to fight me. Not since Montana."

Well, Stark definitely had her attention now. Denver sat up straighter. "He can't Change into his wolf?"

"Nope. Means we have to fight with fists, or it's just not a fair fight. Super boring, but he will get it sorted out when he takes on the Pack bonds."

"That won't fix a broken wolf. It'll make it worse."

"I know."

"Then why are you okay with it?"

"Who said I'm okay with it? You forget your place, fox, and you forget mine as well. I'm here to obey. Tessa says jump, and I say, 'how fuckin' high?'. I can't control what happens to this Pack any more than I can control the pull of the moon." He pointed to the brown paper bag in her hand. "Is that a sack lunch?"

"I made it for Daylen. I used to bring him ham sandwiches at work on his lunch breaks, but..."

"You like him."

That was what everyone had always accused her of. "He's my best friend. Always has been."

"But there's more to it than that. You got loyal."

God, he was obnoxious. "I get loyal to anyone who is kind to me."

"And has he been kind? This past two years, has he been kind?"

She didn't like the direct questions, or feeling like she was being maneuvered into some corner to absorb one of Stark's stupid punchlines. She crossed her arms and looked off into the woods.

"No answer is an answer." His chair creaked under the weight of him leaning back farther into it. "I wouldn't have left you like that."

"Yes, you would've."

"You're right," he said with a chuckle. "It was just fun trying to get away with a lie in front of you."

"I'm too smart for my own good, remember?"

Stark nodded and got a faraway look as he stared off into the woods. "You're too good for what is going to happen."

That sounded very truthful though, so she studied the sharp angles of his face. "What will happen?"

"The Pack is on fire, rolling down a cliff, and our leader is weighing us all down. She has been for the last two years. Daylen was supposed to catch us. Has he told you where he got the scar on his face?"

"No," she whispered.

"You should get that answer before you go back to making him sack lunches." Stark slid his frost-blue gaze to her. "Tessa said we should've never come back here, because of you. And she was right, but not in the way she thinks. She thinks you will drag Daylen down, but he's already down. I think you can save him, but only at the sacrifice of yourself. Either way, someone loses." He shrugged up one shoulder. "You're too good for this shit."

"Was it easy for him?" she asked suddenly. The answer was more important than she ever wanted to admit. "Was it easy for him to leave me, and stay away?"

Stark showed his sharp canines and a snarl rattled his throat. Sure, he talked easy, but inside of him was a titan that Denver had been unlucky enough to see on two occasions. And both were bloody, drawn-out wolf fights between him and Daylen. They'd always hated each other. "It was very easy for him."

Lie. He didn't even try to hide the lie.

"What are you really doing here?" she asked Stark, because things weren't matching up.

"I have nowhere else to go."

Another lie.

And it hit her—this little instinct that said things weren't what they appeared, and perhaps they never had been. "You don't hate Daylen at all, do you?"

Stark leaned forward and his eyes flashed white. "He could die tomorrow and I wouldn't lose an ounce of sleep over it."

Oooh, defensive. "I got a little too close, didn't I?"

"You should go, little fox. Scurry back to your people, where it's safe. You don't belong here."

"Yep," she said, clapping her palms on the armrests of the chair. She stood and gave him a tiny salute. "See ya around, Stark."

And as she drove away, she looked into the rearview mirror and saw him chuck his coffee mug. It shattered against a tree, and then Stark stormed into the woods.

Maybe that wolf had a heart after all, and that gave her a very good, but very dangerous idea.

TWELVE

Her old Dodge huffed up the slushy mountain road, and she had such a feeling of déjà vu as she drove under the Gateway Lumber sign. Daylen had worked here since he was eighteen. Honestly, if he would've stayed, he would've been foreman. Abel had been offering him the second highest job in the yard before Vager got sentenced.

Abel was walking out of the office with a clipboard and mud up to his ankles as she passed him to go park in the side lot. He waved her down.

"Never thought I would see you rolling through here again," he said through a grin.

"It all feels really familiar, doesn't it?"

"It does. It does," he mused. "Except…" He tilted his head toward a forklift. Daylen was working it. "Is he doing all right?"

Denver chewed the side of her mouth and shook her head. "Honestly, I don't know what all is going on, but I think he'll be fine. He's tough."

"Oh, they don't make them any tougher," Abel agreed. "In all my years here, he's the only one that shows up rain, or snow, or shine, and puts his head down and works like hell. He'll do the work of two men and make it look easy. He's just…I don't know. Different now." Abel scratched his gray beard and his brown eyes sparkled as he looked back at her and said, "Get him back on track, will ya?"

"Me?" she asked. "I can't control that boy."

"He ain't a boy anymore. When a boy turns into a man, a good woman can absolutely guide him. He gets mature enough to put his ego aside and let a teammate help." Abel clapped his hand on the open window and gave her a wink. "Ask my wife."

"Tell Sasha hi for me," she called as he walked toward a towering stack of two-by-fours.

"Will do," he said without turning around.

Everyone in this damn town thought she had more of a role in Daylen's life than she actually did. It was weird.

Shaking her head, Denver parked, and thoughtfully watched Daylen work for a few minutes. He hadn't noticed she was here, which was insane because he was a werewolf, and werewolves saw and heard all. It's not like her truck was quiet. The thing was practically coughing the entire way up that mountain road.

He wore a chocolate-brown T-shirt, a belt, and work jeans. His tattoos were stark against his skin, and his hard hat was pulled just low enough over his sunglasses that she could only see the grim set of his lips. His face was frozen like that as he worked, like there was no thought behind those sunglasses.

It was a good five minutes before she shoved the truck door open, grabbed a hardhat from the row of pegs on the side of the office building, and trudged through the slush toward the forklift.

It wasn't until he finished loading an entire shelf of two-by-fours onto a massive trailer that he turned the forklift and saw her there. He startled and the machine under him came to a quick stop.

"Denver?" he asked, but his tone was empty.

She held up the sack lunch. "Lunch break?"

"Yeah. No, wait..."

"I don't give two fucks what Tessa said. Come on."

He huffed a laugh and shook his head. He mumbled something under his breath but the whir of the machine was too loud for her to make it out.

He turned it off, hopped down, and strode toward her, and good gah, that man had upped his attractive points over the past couple years.

Every curve of muscle pushed against his clothes. She could see the perfect line of his chest from here. Hellooooo, Daylen Delicious.

He tried to smile, but his face looked empty. Something was wrong.

"I made your favorite," she told him as he led the way to the picnic table beside the office. Someone had left a soda can on it, and he tossed it into the recycling bin before he took a seat across from her.

"You didn't have to do that." God, his words were so monotone.

"Hey," she said, reaching across the table. She touched his hand, and he just stared at it. "Are you good?"

"Good?" He pulled his hand away and removed his hard hat. "No. I'm not good."

Truth.

"What's going on?"

"I can't feel anything. When you aren't around, I don't...there's just...nothing."

"What happened to your wolf, Daylen? Stark

said you can't Change. What happened to him?"

Daylen clasped his hands on the table and shook his head back and forth, back and forth.

Done with the sunglasses that hid his eyes, she reached forward and pulled them off gently. When he looked up, his eyes were blazing the gold of his wolf, but he just smelled like a man.

"Ham?" he guessed as he busied himself pulling out sandwiches.

She'd made four. Three for him and one for her.

He needed her to change the subject. Maybe that would bring him back to life a little.

"I saw Stark's campsite."

"Oh geez. He's the worst."

"Remember that time he got you in that huge fight at Rowdy's?"

Daylen's eyes sparked with a little bit of life. "You started all of that."

"Me?" she asked innocently. Denver scarfed a big bite, and around it she said, "I don't know what you're talking about. I was just an innocent bystander."

Daylen snorted. "You punched that dude's girlfriend."

"Because she tripped me."

"And then you told her...and I quote... 'I can take your pussy boyfriend, too.' And then Stark laughed, and he shoved the dude, and that dude had what...four friends with him? And all I wanted to do was chill and watch the damn fireworks, but no. You and Stark started a war with half the town that night."

"I'm adorable."

He laughed softly. "I don't know if adorable is the right word. You didn't want to go home that night, so you stole my bed and made me sleep on the couch. And you stole my favorite T-shirt to sleep in and never gave it back. You still owe me a Coors Banquet shirt, by the way."

"I have an admission about that night."

"Oh God."

"I totally saw your...you know." Heat burned up her neck and landed in her cheeks, and she couldn't hold his shocked gaze.

"You saw my what?" he demanded.

"You know...your wiener."

"My wiener? Never call it a wiener again, Denver. You just sucked all the masculinity from me in one word."

"I saw your pea shooter."

"Stop," he said, trying to hide a grin.

"Your gravy bazooka. Your meaty arm. Your—"

"Okay! That's good. How..." He cleared his throat and lowered his voice. "How did you see it?"

"You sleep bare-ass naked. When you got up to go take a shower the next morning, you walked right in front of the doorway to your room, and I was awake enough to see your...morning wood."

"Shoot me."

"It's huge."

"So how was your morning?" he asked, trying to change the subject.

"I feel like as friends, we should get all the awkwardness out of the way."

"Probably should've tackled that ten years ago when it happened."

"Stark is even weirder than I remember," she said.

"I saw your tits," he uttered.

"What?"

"You were getting dressed in my T-shirt that night, and I didn't know you were changing. I came in to bring you food, and I saw your profile, and that's why that morning wood happened. I couldn't stop thinking about the way you looked all night. I had like three dirty dreams about you. I felt like a horrible person."

"Wh-why?"

"Because I wasn't supposed to be lusting over my best friend. Don't tell my dick that though. I was confused for a week after that."

She belted out a laugh that echoed through the lumberyard. "This is awesome."

"Disagree."

"Look, it's normal that we saw each other naked at some point. We spent so much dang time together. Plus, how many times did we have slumber parties? A hundred? You're really telling me that's the only time you saw me naked?"

He pursed his lips, but it didn't hide the tiny naughty smile tugging at the corners.

"You know what I think?" she asked after they ate for a couple of minutes.

"There's no telling what you're thinking, ever," he muttered.

"I think you need to have some fun."

"I can't Change," he said, looking confused.

"Boy, is that the only fun you know how to have? Going wolf? He'll come back, but until then, you need to do some self-care on the man. Look at it like a blessing in disguise. Your entire life has revolved around caring for the bloodthirsty side of you. If he's quiet? Good. Let's get back to the basics."

"The basics," he repeated, one eyebrow arched up.

She counted them off on her fingers. "Beer, babes, good food, earning that steak after a hard days' work, snow hikes, visit the places that used to make you happy, get to know the new you."

He looked skeptical. "You think it's a good idea to unleash me on the babes of this town?"

"Hmm. Yeah, you're kind of crazy right now. Maybe we will wait on the babes."

He lifted his chin a little higher and narrowed his eyes at her. "Crazy? Says the one who set a huge fire on my front lawn. Also, your fox pissed all over my woods."

Denver shrugged unapologetically. "They were her woods for a while."

"Did you go to my house this morning?"

"Yep."

"Did you notice the front door?"

Denver frowned. "No. What's wrong with it?"

"There's a new dog bed by it." He took a big bite of sandwich. Oh, there was a lot of life in those eyes now.

"I think Tessa doesn't need to have a say in

your life anymore, Daylen."

"She's my Alpha—"

"Not a good one. And more than that? She is your mother. Because she's both, she blurred the lines of loyalty for you, and I can see you getting trapped. Vager was trapped, too."

The smile fell off his face like it had never existed at all. "Don't talk about things you don't understand."

"Don't I understand, though? My animal can't even stand to be inside a house for more than a minute, two minutes tops. And Vager got caught making a kill and he got thrown behind bars, and that's about as trapped as I could imagine. Until now."

"I'm not trapped."

"I bet his eyes went dead like yours do."

"Fuck, Denver. Can I escape it for five goddamn minutes? I'm tired of being inside my head. You're an escape, but if you keep digging at things that need to stay buried, you aren't going to be an escape at all. You're going to be part of the problem."

"Or," she said, standing to come sit on his side of the picnic table, right by him. "You have some infected wounds inside of there," she said, pointing to his head. "And you need someone to come in, open them up, and clear out the grit. Lucky for you, I've seen you at your worst and I don't mind doing the dirty work."

Daylen had gone quiet and still. His gold eyes locked onto hers, intensity sparking in his look. He swallowed hard. "You aren't going to quit on me, are you?"

"Never." It was a quick answer. An easy one, and she let that man hear the honesty in her tone. "You're my best friend."

His gaze dipped to her lips, and suddenly she became hyperaware of how close she was sitting to him.

She'd done this a million times, sat this close to Daylen, but this time was different. There was something hungry about him. Desperate maybe. A loud head sometimes searched for something happy, and she knew her capabilities. She could be his happy.

But this time, she had been recognizing how handsome he looked. How different he felt. How mysterious, how grown up. She'd realized the battle he was fighting, and her heart had started cheering him on in a different way. Only it wasn't until this very moment, right here, trapped in that blazing gaze of his, that she realized he really was her best friend, but more.

Her fox had gone still and watchful inside of her chest, and filled her with a yearning she'd never had before.

Daylen was so big, so strong. Tough. A man of few words who had shouldered the weight of the world for so long, and made it look easy.

Heart hammering in her chest, she leaned forward by an inch, testing, confused, expecting him to push her in the snow and laugh at her.

But he didn't.

Instead, he leaned in and slid his hand to the back of her neck as he pressed his lips to hers.

Friends didn't kiss, not like this. He dragged her waist closer and his grip on her neck tightened as his lips moved against hers. And God, he tasted good, and his mouth was so warm against hers. When he pushed his tongue past her lips and brushed it lightly against hers, she gave in and melted into him.

When he released her, his breath was shaking right along with hers.

He looked as confused as she felt.

"I shouldn't have done that," he murmured in a gruff voice. "I'm sorry."

She searched her soul for any guilty feelings, or the sensation of wrongness, but none existed.

Denver smiled and huffed a breath. "Don't be," she whispered.

Releasing his shirt from her grip, she brushed a finger down his new scar.

His eyes went round and he flinched back. With a gasp, he stood in a rush. "I have to get back to work."

She could smell the panic on him, could feel it

coming off him in waves.

"Wait, Daylen!"

He snatched his hard hat and jogged off, disappeared behind a huge stack of lumber, and left her feeling like she was the one on fire, falling down the cliff.

It was the best kiss she'd ever had, but it had ruined everything. Destroyed any progress. Set them back miles.

Something was wrong with Daylen, and that hadn't helped him.

You're going to be part of the problem.

Denver touched her throbbing lips lightly.

Every part of her body was reaching toward him, but that wolf had something going on that she didn't understand. For the first time in her life, she felt like she didn't know how to be there for him. Like perhaps she didn't know him anymore.

Denver did know one thing though.

She was tired of missing him.

THIRTEEN

The last two days since Denver had seen Daylen at the lumberyard had been extremely quiet.

Her job was easy. She'd been an assistant to the town's only doctor for the last ten years. Since Denver wasn't a nurse, she couldn't help treat patients, but she was in charge of scheduling appointments, ordering supplies, inventory, patient paperwork, and making sure Dr. Brakeen ate every once in a while. There were slow days in such a small town. There were also very busy days that dragged into the night, depending on what catastrophe occurred, but they were like a well-oiled machine after working together for so long.

Today had been one of the catastrophe days.

One of the farmers that lived outside of town had decided to trim tree limbs that were hanging heavy with ice and fell thirty feet down, breaking his arm, his ribs, and one of his ankles. His wife had gone to work without knowing he was going to execute his man plan. He wasn't even wearing a safety harness or anything. Silly human males.

He'd been brought in right at close, and the doctor had to stabilize him before they could transport him to a hospital. His wife had brought him to the office because the man was howling about how he wouldn't see anyone but Dr. Brakeen, and he'd be damned if he let the hospital take his life savings.

She was tired to her bones.

Denver pulled up the snowy drive to her home but stopped short of her parking spot in front of the house. Why? Because there was already a truck parked there—an old Chevy Silverado, with a certain werewolf leaning against it. He had a six-pack of bottled RC Cola in one hand and a family-sized bag of Cheetos in the other.

She parked where she was and got out. "Those are my favorite snacks," she said carefully.

"I remember."

Denver tipped her chin higher into the air. "Why are you here?"

"To say I'm sorry."

"Daylen Hoda, that's all you do anymore." She marched right past his truck, changed her mind, and turned to yank the bag of Cheetos from his hand. "Thank you."

"So, you forgive me?" he asked, following her.

"For what? For kissing me and then freaking out and making things all awkward between us? Or for being weird and dodging every serious question I ask?"

"Denver, I need one night."

147

She narrowed her eyes. "Is this a booty call?"

"No! God, no. No, no, no, the kiss was a mistake! It was a lapse in judgement, and I wasn't in my right mind and it's...it's...you! Denver, it's you and you've always been there and you're...you're...you're just you! And I lost my head and kissed you and it wasn't a bad kiss." He looked panicked and ran his hands through his hair until it stuck up everywhere. How did he still look perfect with messy hair? Obnoxious. "It was a good kiss. I mean as far as that stuff goes...you're great! But I need one normal night where I can just be around you like old times and there is nothing to work on and there is nothing to catch up on and there is no awkwardness." He sighed heavily, and she could see it—the exhaustion etched into his face.

Denver hugged the bag of Cheetos to her chest and twitched her head toward the door. "I could go for pizza and a Buffy the Vampire Slayer marathon tonight."

She'd never witnessed such potent relief on a

man's face before.

"No talking about the past unless it's happy. No serious talk at all. And absolutely no mentioning that kiss," she said, making the rules that would put him at ease.

"It was a stupid kiss," he murmured.

"So dumb. I haven't thought about it even one time."

His lips quirked up into a crooked smile. "Liar."

She shrugged up a shoulder unapologetically and led the way inside. "Come on best friend, we have pizza to order. I'm getting the shrimp special."

"No one makes pizza with shrimp on it," he muttered as he removed his snowy boots in her entryway.

"Well, they should," she told him as she connected a call to the local pizza place. She ordered two pepperoni pizzas, a meat lover's pizza, cheese sticks, and chicken wings with extra ranch because she knew exactly how much a werewolf could eat. "Forty minutes," she told Daylen, who was helping himself to a tour of her little two-bedroom home.

"You always made us watch Buffy when you were mad at me," he called from the back bedroom.

"Best punishment ever. That show is awesome." She poured a couple of the RC colas into ice-filled glasses and pulled a couple of candy options from her sweets stash, then set it all up in the living room.

"This place looks way different than I thought it would," he mused as he came back into the living room. He'd probably sniffed out every corner. His wolf had always demanded he know all the entrances and exits in an enclosed building before he could relax.

"Honestly, it looks way different than when I bought it last year. I repainted everything and ripped out all the old, dirty carpet. I was going to put vinyl flooring down, but realized it had hardwood underneath, so I hired someone to sand it down and re-stain it."

He looked around with an impressed arch to his eyebrow.

She retrieved all the pillows she could find, and two huge quilts, and tossed them at him on the couch. He spread all that out and made little nests while she dug through her DVD collection to find season one. She took her favorite spot on the ground in front of the couch, leaning back on it, and he took the couch.

How many hundreds of times had they sat just like this over the years they'd known each other?

When she caught him staring at her, she smiled up at him. "This feels good."

His full lips curved up into a grin that she had thought she would never see again. He patted her head like she was a dog and relaxed back onto her couch. "I never understood why you didn't like sitting up on the couch with me," he mused as the intro began to play.

"Oh, that's an obvious one. Your wolf is a

demon and requires everyone around him to submit."

"Bullshit," he said. "I could be a dragon shifter and you still wouldn't submit."

"Wanna bet? I'm not submissive in general, but I'm smart. When your wolf gets testy, so do you."

He frowned at her. "What do you mean?"

"I can feel everything he feels. I can practically smell his emotions, and your attitude follows. Except for now," she said as she pulled her knees up to her chest. "Right now, I can barely smell him at all."

"And yet you still sit down there."

"Reason number two I sit down here—you always fall asleep and hog the whole couch."

"Well, you're safe from that now. I don't sleep anymore."

"Oh, you've turned into a vampire? I'm telling Buffy."

He snorted and shook his head. "No, it's bad dreams or something. I can pass out for maybe fifteen minutes at a time. Denver?" he said suddenly. "I'm Alpha now. It happened tonight."

Denver's mouth fell open. Slowly, she turned so she could see him better. Resting her side against the couch, she asked, "Why aren't you celebrating with the Pack?"

He shook his head, his fiery gold eyes locked onto hers. His expression said the words his mouth would not. There was nothing to celebrate.

But to her, there was. Being Alpha was a tremendous honor. He would be the leader in this territory for many years to come. He. Was. King.

She cracked a smile and hoisted herself onto the edge of the couch, and with only a three-count of hesitation, she slid her arms around his waist and hugged him as tight as she could. "Congratulations, Daylen."

"What?"

She shoved him back to arm's length and shook his shoulders gently. "You're Alpha.

Alpha."

He was looking at her like she'd lost her mind. "Alpha in place of my brother, and I only have two wolves under me. One is Stark, the village idiot of the werewolf community, and he's on his last chance before an Alpha has to put him down." Daylen pointed at himself. "Me. I'm the Alpha who gets to do that. And then there's Marsden, who has barely strung two words together in the last twelve months, and is currently going wolf about eight times a day. He threw a tomahawk at me today when I asked him to be the Alpha instead. A tomahawk, Denver. Where the fuck did he even get a tomahawk?"

She was trying not to laugh. Truly she was, but it was kind of funny that he inherited the most fucked up werewolf Pack in existence.

"Okay, but bright side, if you're Alpha it means no one, aka Tessa, is Alpha over you."

"Yeah, well, she's on a rampage because my first act as Alpha was to kick her out of the Pack."

The laugh-snort that escaped her throat

wasn't her fault. It really wasn't. She hadn't realized until this very moment that she'd been waiting years for Tessa to get a dose of her own medicine.

"This is amazing," she burst out. "Wait!" She hit pause on the show and snuggled onto the couch cushion across from him with her soda, took a slurp, and then said, "Tell me all the dirt."

"None of this is funny," he muttered.

"It's a little funny. What did Tessa's face look like when you said it? Did her eye twitch? Wait! Start at the beginning. What were the exact words you used?"

"Uuuuh...she called a meeting at her house and said she was done with all of our shit, and that I needed to step up and take responsibility for the empire she'd built for me. Stark started laughing really hard, and Tessa got angrier somehow, which was impressive, because I didn't think she could physically get any madder. Then Marsden said he should've left with everyone else, and Tessa said I was supposed to fight her because it was tradition that the former Alpha pass the torch to the new one with bloodshed. I told her to imagine the fight because I'm not doing that shit, and then I asked Marsden to go fight her, and he called me a fuckworm, whatever that means. I told him, 'no, really, you should be Alpha', and he threw a tomahawk at my face. I ducked out of the way, and it sank into the urn holding my dad's ashes. The ashes exploded everywhere, and got into my mouth, and Stark wouldn't stop laughing. Tessa was screaming and trying to scoop my dad's ashes back into the broken urn, and Marsden asked why did she even keep the ashes of a man she hated, and then he stormed out of the house. Tessa said she didn't give a fuck what I wanted, I'm Alpha now and I can just deal with it. Then she did some awful magic shit to my head and now I can physically feel Stark and Marsden's bonds to me. I had this headache and Tessa was screaming about how we'd fucked everything up, and Stark told me she was a pill and I should just kick her out of the Pack. That sounded pretty damn awesome right about then, so I told her to leave, and that's the story about how I accidentally ate my dad and made Tessa leave her own house. It was my first order. Pretty sure I'm nailing this. And when I walked outside hacking and coughing because those freaking ashes were brutal, Stark came out after me and I'm pretty sure he tried to strangle me, so I pushed him off me and got in my truck and drove straight to the gas station to get you some RC Cola and Cheetos and wash my damn face and arms in the restroom before I came here. You know how everyone says werewolves are crazy?"

She nodded, a grin plastered to her face because this was the greatest story she'd ever heard.

"They're right. We're fucking crazy."

"All right, bright sides—"

"Oh my God. Denver, there are no bright sides to this."

"You barely even met your dad, so choking on his ashes isn't that bad." She was really trying not to laugh as she made her way through this. "Bright side number two, I'm pretty sure Stark wasn't trying to strangle you. He was probably trying to hug you. He just has the emotional maturity of a slug and it probably looked like strangling. That boy probably hasn't had a hug in his entire life. Three, Marsden didn't actually hit you with the tomahawk. If he wanted you dead, you would be dead. Four. There's probably worse Packs out there."

"Name one," Daylen deadpanned.

"Well..." Crap, she knew of most of the Packs because Daylen had always given her the dirt on them, but really, even the craziest ones were better off than this one right now. "Then you'll get the most improved award. Eeeh?" She waggled her eyebrows. "It's only up from here. And last but not least, you can change the Pack name. No more Sheridan Pack. That was your mother's maiden name. It was her legacy. You get to start making your own legacy. We can come up with a badass name!"

"The Three Psychopaths," he muttered.

"No! It has to be something meaningful. Something cool."

His eye twitched.

"Look, I know this wasn't the path you wanted. I know it. I've watched you struggle against the Pack all of your life, but things went sideways, Daylen. Vager couldn't take the Pack, so you have to take on the work for him. Who cares what Tessa thinks? What would Vager want? Build this Pack into something he would be proud of, something that pays tribute to him. But even more importantly? Build the Pack into something *you* can be proud of."

The disdain melted from his face, and the tightness around his eyes and lips softened.

"Build the Pack I want," he murmured softly.

"Who said you can't? Where is the rule book that says that?"

There was a slow smile that spread across his

face. "You were always dangerous."

"Hell yeah I am. I have sharp teeth." She started making chomping noises, but he stopped her.

"No, it's not just because of your fox. You live outside of the Pack and by your own rules—"

"Wrong. I live by fox rules."

"No, you don't. When have you ever minded the rules your parents put in place?"

"Right now. I'm talking to Bartholomew, like they asked." Kind of. Truth be told, she hadn't messaged him back after his multiple girlfriend revelation.

Daylen glared at her thoughtfully. "He's never been here, to your den. I don't smell anyone in here but you."

Aaaah, that's why he'd been sniffing around the rooms earlier. "Maybe he's coming over tomorrow," she said cheekily.

His chuckle was downright dark, and his eyes flashed brighter gold. "Stop playing, Denver."

She didn't understand. He'd gone serious so

fast. She put her bare foot onto the side of his leg and pushed. It worked to break that ice he'd built in an instant, because he relaxed back onto the couch, but he did something that shocked her to her bones. Daylen pulled her foot into his lap and began to massage the arch, and good Lord, she'd never felt anything better. No one had ever been allowed to touch her like this, but it was Daylen. She trusted him with everything.

She groaned helplessly and went to mush against the cushions. A tornado could hit this house right now and she wouldn't even notice.

"Look at us, Daylen," she murmured. "Just look. The Alpha of the Bagel Bite Pack massaging a lowly fox shifter's feet. My mojo must be epic."

He belted out a laugh and vetoed the name she'd come up with. He moved to her other foot, and she didn't even know what was happening to her body right now.

"You're fun," he said after a few minutes. "I can tell exactly what you like because you're noisy about it."

Was she? Denver eased her eyes open and halted the purring sound in her throat. Well, that was embarrassing. Daylen was looking back at her with this intensity she'd never witnessed on his face before. He was different now. Darker, and more mysterious, and full of this raw sex appeal she'd never noticed before. Oh, she'd noticed he was handsome, and had watched the other girls in town fawn all over him when they'd been growing up, but he'd always just been Daylen to her.

Daylen, the werewolf.

Daylen, her best friend.

Daylen, the untouchable.

But now? He ran his thumb firmly down the length of the arch of her foot and made her feel boneless. He seemed touchable enough.

She didn't know what her face was saying to him right now, but he dragged his attention to her lips and back up to her eyes, and the wicked glint in his expression made her stomach do strange flip-flops.

She thought about the kiss he'd given her. How could she not? She'd replayed it a hundred times over the last couple of days. It had been some kind of forbidden fruit she hadn't realized she wanted, and now that she'd tasted it, she couldn't stop thinking about it.

But he was a friend.

A friend, a friend, a friend. She'd watched him through all of his awkward teenage years, and he'd seen hers as well. They were just friends. Always had been...always would be.

Daylen's lips curled back in a feral smile and he released her foot, crawled over her and hovered there, his sheer size blocking out the entire ceiling above.

He searched her eyes. "I always liked when the fox was right at the surface," he rumbled in a snarling voice she'd rarely heard from him. He brushed his finger lightly under her eye, and her breath froze in her chest.

The flip-flops in her stomach turned to an angry bee hive, and her body yearned for the warmth of his.

She clutched his shirt as he leaned down, and just before his lips touched hers, he hesitated.

Her breath shook in the moment he hovered there, millimeters from her lips. And when he leaned in the rest of the way and pressed his mouth to hers, she let off one of those helpless little purrs again.

The noise seemed to affect Daylen, and his control slipped. His kiss hardened, and his teeth scraped her lips. He lowered his body to hers and they caught fire. It's the only way she could describe it. They were a forest fire, uncontrollable, burning against each other, frenzied movement and heat that consumed her.

He pushed her knees apart and settled in between her inner thighs, and she could feel his hard dick pressing against the zipper of his jeans. Oooh, it felt so good. His kiss was everything, ravaging her, destroying all logic she had until she was mindless friction against him. He rolled his body against hers and she met him, held him tight, kissed him just as violently as he was kissing her.

"Fuck," he growled, thrusting powerfully against her. He ran his hand up under her shirt and slipped it under her bra, and then groaned the most desperate, sexy sound she'd ever heard.

She was gone. He could have it. Have it, have her, have everything.

He pulled his mouth from hers and pressed a gentle bite against her throat as he rocked against her.

More, more, more! Denver shoved the hem of his shirt upward and he pulled it off in a rush before he lowered back down. She could feel his skin against her now. He was burning up.

Knock, knock, knock.

Daylen froze, his arms locked on either side of her face, abs flexing with his breath, eyes the color of golden fire.

He pushed off her in a rush and was to the other side of the room in an instant. He blurred with the movement. "Someone is at the door."

"P-pizza," she huffed out.

He shook his head and she could see it now—the panic in his eyes. "We can't do this."

Her breath was shaking. She'd lost her mind. With Daylen. With her best friend. "I understand." She most definitely did not understand.

"It's not you," he rushed out. "It's just. I—" He paced to the hallway and back, running his hands roughly through his hair. "You're more than this. More than just a need. You're better. I'm a fucking mess right now, and you deserve for me to be more careful."

Knock, knock.

He growled and pulled his wallet from his back pocket. "I'll get the pizza."

"Don't run," she told him. "I'll take a minute and then we will come back to our pizza night and pretend that didn't just happen. I just don't want you to run anymore."

He nodded, and his lips parted like he wanted to say more, but he changed his mind and sauntered to the door.

Denver needed a minute to pull herself together. One look at her reflection in the bathroom mirror and she giggled. "Oh my goodness, Denver Agatha Mosely, what has that boy done to you?" she whispered to herself.

Her curly hair was a rat's nest on one side, her cheeks were flushed bright pink, her lips were swollen, and he'd nipped her neck harder than she'd thought because there was definitely a mark there. Her nipples were perked up against the inside of her bra, and her entire body was still wanting. And she understood what he was saying about her eyes. The gold fox eyes were right there and couldn't be mistaken for human.

Denver brushed her fingers quickly through her hair and straightened her shirt, all the while hiding a smile. She was supposed to regret what she and Daylen had just done, because they were just friends and blah, blah, blah. But right now, her fox was downright giddy and her hormones were raging. If she was really lucky, when she went back to the living room, he would still be shirtless.

Daylen. Was. So. Dang. Sexy.

She moseyed on out to the living room, following the scent of pepperoni and cheese, and her face fell in disappointment.

Hottie Daylen had definitely put his shirt back on. Lame.

She'd always been comfortable with the friendzone until tonight, when she'd taken a swan dive off of Make-Out Mountain and straight into Daylen-Has-A-Big-Boner Lake.

"Hello, friend," he greeted her with a baiting smile.

"Crucial announcement: my hair was a mess," she illuminated him, like he hadn't seen it and probably gave her an out to fix herself because she looked like she'd been through a category three tornado.

"If we weren't just friends, I would've liked it messy like that, and I would also enjoy the way you smell like sex right now, but neither of those things matter because we are just friends and I don't notice such things," he told her as he piled pizza slices onto a paper plate. He handed it to her.

Boys with crooked smiles were dangerous.

Primly, she lifted her chin into the air, accepted the plate, and took the seat on the couch across from him as he hit the play button. And that boy sat over there, a mile away from her, and ate his food comfortably. He even snorted and chuckled at the appropriate parts of the show like they hadn't just changed the entire makeup of their friendship. And all the while she sat there, hyperaware of his every move and completely unable to pay attention to the greatest show in the world.

That's what cute boys did. They sucked all the focus from a room, and she, Denver Agatha Mosley, needed to get her act together.

She needed to have a serious talk with him, even though it was against the rules of the night.

Daylen, I'm growing a crush on you because you kissed the devil out of me and now I can't even see straight because my stupid eyeballs just want to drift to you. Also, I really like your erection. God, don't say erection. Boner. Hardened member? Snausage. Wow, what an elite vocabulary. Peckerwood. I like your peckerwood? It had been a very long time since she'd tried to define a relationship with a boy.

She turned to ask him if he preferred to have his dick referred to as a peener, or a ptero-dick-tyl, but he was resting his head on his hand on the arm of the couch and was sound asleep.

He'd said he couldn't sleep much lately. Maybe fifteen minutes at a time, and he was probably exhausted from stress and moving and settling back into his life here and work and being awesome at making out.

So, she tiptoed to her bedroom and grabbed her softest pillow, dragged it back into the living room, gently pressed it under his cheek, and then tucked him in.

Big, tough, murdery werewolf didn't need to be tucked in by anyone, but she wasn't just anyone. He was safe here.

She stood back and watched his face relax in his sleep, and it struck her how tense he'd looked since he'd come back home. That man was carrying a weight on his shoulders she couldn't imagine, and without the shadow of a doubt, she knew he was keeping secrets.

Stark had told her to figure out where the scar on his face had come from. Over the last couple of days, since she'd touched it at the lumberyard and he'd freaked out, she hadn't been able to stop imagining the worst. He must've killed one of the Pack members. Or maybe all of them. All the for-sale signs in all those yards. Werewolves didn't talk about kills. It was one of their rules. They didn't talk about them, but rare was an old werewolf who hadn't killed in his lifetime. Packs fought savagely over territory, and for hierarchy within the Pack, and sometimes they just lost control and didn't curb their strength in fights with humans. Like Vager had done in that stupid bar fight that had gotten him locked away.

What was Daylen's story?

She knelt down and studied his face. Sharp jawline, chiseled cheeks, and full lips. If he opened his eyes right now, they would be gold. She loved the color of his eyes, but she'd never told him that. She'd never told him she found him attractive at all. That was against the unspoken rules of their friendship.

Everything between them had worked if they didn't bring deep feelings into their friendship.

And now there was no turning back—at least for her. He'd ruined that by awakening her heart with that kiss.

She'd really, really missed him over the last two years, but maybe her fox had been heartbroken for deeper reasons. Maybe she'd been obsessed with spending time in his abandoned territory because she needed to fill the giant hole he'd left in her.

Stark said she'd gotten loyal, and he was right.

Over the years, she had become irreversibly loyal to Daylen.

She was a mess.

With a soft sigh, she stood and cuddled up on the other side of the couch, carefully pulled the blanket over herself, and rested her cheek against the throw pillow.

Daylen was safe here with her, and she knew she was safe, too.

It was fifteen little minutes before Daylen would wake up, and she would watch over him until then.

****

Movement behind her startled Denver awake, but one sniff of the air and her fox settled. It was Daylen. Sleepy Daylen. He smelled different, and so good when he was tired. It settled something within her. He was maneuvering the soft pillow under her head.

One glance at the clock on the kitchen

microwave, and she gave a sleepy smile. "Did you sleep?" she whispered.

"Like the dead. It's four in the morning."

His voice was deep and rumbling, and the velvet gravel of it lulled her into relaxing even more. "My alarm won't go off until six." She was still whispering because she didn't want to shake up the magic of this moment. He was fidgeting with her pillow, making it just right...she did that too, before sleep. She nested. But he was doing it for her, fussing with the pillow, tucking the blanket it around her just so...

It was dark outside, and he'd turned off all of the lights except for the undermount lighting under the kitchen cabinets. It cast the living room in a dim, warm glow, and highlighted the chiseled lines of his handsome face.

"I slept," he told her again.

"You can sleep more."

He knelt in front of her and cocked his head like a curious animal. His eyes were glowing against the dark. "There are wolves outside."

Her breath caught, and she moved to get up.

"No, no," he murmured, pressing his hand against her shoulder to keep her in place. "It's just Stark and Marsden."

Oh. Not Tessa, then. Stark and Marsden wouldn't try to kill her. Probably.

"Do you have to go?" she asked. Maybe she was pouting a little.

He huffed a tiny laugh, and she could see the smile lines around his mouth. Handsome boy. "You want me to stay until you fall back asleep?"

She nodded.

Denver thought he would go back to his side of the couch, but he stunned her completely by snuggling in behind her. She scooted forward automatically to make more room for his massive body, and yeah, she was hanging halfway off the couch, but she was fine with it because Daylen slid his hands around her and held her in place.

His heart was drumming double-time against her back. It felt right. It felt natural. Denver relaxed into him.

"You purr a lot now," he murmured against the back of her hair.

"You'd think I had a cat in me," she said sleepily.

"I like that noise," he admitted so softly she almost missed it. "Means you're happy."

And she was. In moments like these, she truly was. He was back. He was better than she remembered. He was attentive and building something in her she would've never expected.

And there in the early morning hours, surrounded by Daylen, hugged up tight where the wolves outside her door could never reach her, she drifted off to sleep again.

FOURTEEN

"You shouldn't be here," Daylen growled at Stark as he pulled his jacket on in the frosty dawn air.

"No, *you* shouldn't be here," Stark retorted like the annoying little thorn he was. "We need a ride back."

"Dude, you're bare-ass naked. You aren't getting your balls on my seats. Where are your damn clothes?" he snapped as Stark cupped his dick and trotted after him.

"Me and Marsden ran all the way from your property to here. As wolves. Obviously."

Daylen ignored him and continued on toward his truck.

"Wolves don't wear clothes, *Daylen*," Stark said loudly.

"Shhhhh! Shh, shh, shut...up!" Daylen hissed out. "You're going to wake Denver."

"We've been out here freezing our nuts off for you," Marsden growled as he yanked open the passenger-side door and slid inside. Butt...naked.

"Get out of my truck, Marsden," Daylen growled.

It was downright entertaining watching Marsden slide out of the truck unwillingly. He clung to the seat and the dashboard for a few seconds, but he couldn't fight an Alpha order. "I'm going to eat you," he choked out just before he hit the snow.

Stark shoved Daylen in the shoulder.

"Don't," Daylen snarled.

"You suck as an Alpha."

"No, shit, Sherlock. I was always going to suck. I've been trying to tell all of you that."

Daylen climbed in behind the wheel, leaned over the bench seat, and yanked the passenger door closed as Marsden came to stand beside Stark.

"You owe us," Marsden said.

"Owe you for what?" Daylen demanded.

"Forget it," Stark said to Marsden. "He's shit and he'll always be shit, and he won't see anything but that goddamn scar on his face. Everything else is invisible, so what's the point?"

Marsden dropped his gaze, but Stark's blazing blue eyes stayed trained on Daylen.

Daylen looked to the peaceful serenity of Denver's home, then back to Stark. Why were they in these woods, and why hadn't they knocked or called for him? They'd been out here for an hour, at least.

He swallowed the growl of frustration that threatened to claw up the back of his throat, and softer, he asked, "Why do I owe you?"

"We weren't here to fuck with you," Stark gritted out. "Tessa was in these woods last night."

"We figured you would want us to keep her off the fox," Marsden murmured, eyes still downcast.

"How did you know she would come here?" Daylen asked, already knowing the answer. The boys were smart enough.

"It's her only move," Stark said.

Truth be told, half of Daylen had showed up here to Denver's house because he'd needed her to calm him down and tell him everything was all right, but the other half? Well, that half was the wolf, and he knew Tessa. She'd been his Alpha for a long time. Daylen would've come even if he didn't need reassurance from Denver. He would've come to make sure the she-wolf left her alone.

Never had he thought to ask the boys to team up. They'd never been a team before.

He rubbed his eyes and muttered, "Get in."

"Yesss," Stark said as he and Marsden jogged around the car to hop in the passenger side.

"In the back," Daylen said. "I'm serious about not getting your nut-germs in my truck."

"God, you're such an asshole," Stark griped as he hopped over the back.

"Good morning, boys," Denver called out from her front porch, where she was now leaning against the railing with a big blanket around her shoulders and a megawatt grin across her entire face.

"Morning," Marsden said, hunkering down in the back.

At least he had some modesty. Stark stood there with his legs splayed and his hands on his hips. "Mornin', foxy lady. Hey listen, if Daylen's micro-penis is too small for you, I would be happy to—"

Daylen hit the gas and Stark nearly fell out of the bed of the truck. He barely caught himself on the tailgate.

Denver cracked up, and God, she sure looked pretty in the morning light—all happy, her eyes dancing, and the curls in her hair bouncing with her laughter.

"You guys be sure to make good decisions today," she said with a wave as they pulled away.

"Wouldn't dream of it," Daylen called through his open window.

"Good decisions are for wussies," Stark yelled over the noise of the engine. "He'll text you later!" It was so damn annoying when he pitched his voice up high like that.

Daylen counted to three for patience, and then looked in the rearview mirror so he could see Denver one last time before he curved down the driveway into the trees.

Stark's stupid grinning face was right there, blocking his view. "Are you two going to have babies?"

Daylen slammed on the brakes and Stark's face smacked into the window. "Owww," he groused, holding his nose, but at least the dumbass sat down and left Daylen alone for the few miles back to his house.

He had to get to work soon, so he left the

boys to find their way in life and rushed for the shower. Lunch was going to be light today because he needed to go to the grocery store, but as he was making his BLT sandwiches, he paused and glared out the window. He couldn't stop thinking about those damn words, *you owe us*.

Stark and Marsden didn't have to come out to Denver's place and put up a wall of defense, so why had they?

If Stark really had stuck around just to watch him fail, as he'd said, then why were they out there making sure Tessa didn't go after Denver?

A snarl rattled his throat. He didn't like this *feeling* nonsense. It was uncomfortable and irritating.

He would pay the debt. Daylen slapped four more pieces of bread onto the cutting board and made a couple of extra sandwiches. Bacon, lettuce, tomato, mayo, a little seasoning, and he shoved them into sandwich baggies and then into a couple of brown paper bags. One for each idiot in his Pack.

Highly annoyed with the soft spot that had formed in his stupid heart, he stomped outside and stopped in front of Stark, who was boiling a pot of coffee over the open fire he'd made in Daylen's front yard. What a thorn.

"Where's Marsden?" he grumbled.

Stark narrowed his eyes. "He left. Why?"

Daylen tossed Stark both of the lunch bags and then strode for his truck.

The crinkle of paper rang out through the early morning quiet of the woods, and audibly, Stark sniffed. "I smell lettuce."

"So?" Daylen snipped as he opened his door.

"So, I'm a werewolf. I don't eat rabbit food."

"You get what you get," Daylen said in agitation, and then got in.

"Do you want to fight?" Stark called.

Do I want to fight? Daylen rolled down the window. "What?"

"In return for the food. This is like a present, right? Do you want one back?"

"You think a fight is a present?"

Stark shrugged one shoulder up to his ear and looked truly confused. "Yes?"

Denver had been right. Stark was emotionally constipated.

"No thanks. Please move your tent somewhere else."

"Sure thing. I'll move it over there." He pointed a few yards away and grinned. "See you when you get home."

Daylen clenched his teeth tightly closed to avoid giving in to his goading. It would get him nowhere but frustrated.

You did good.

Daylen slammed on the brakes and his heart rate kicked up at the shock that rang through him.

"What?" he asked the wolf, but the animal was quiet inside of him. Chills rippled up his spine, and he clenched the steering wheel tighter. "What did you say?" he whispered, desperate to hear the voice that had been gone for so long.

Silence.

"Come back," he whispered.

He looked up into the review mirror, but he couldn't see anything but those gold eyes and that damn scar that ran down his face. He ripped his gaze away and slammed his head back against the rest, then eased onto the gas.

He'd imagined it. He'd imagined the wolf's voice telling him he'd done good, because he was desperate to feel less broken. That was all.

It was just his mind playing tricks on him. Had to be.

FIFTEEN

Dr. Brakeen stuck his head into the file room and gave Denver a little wave.

She stopped flipping through the filing cabinet. "Hi," she said around the pencil in her mouth. "I'm almost done. Did the phone ring?" She hadn't heard it, but she was also very distracted today by a certain sexy werewolf that was completely consuming her mind.

"No, no, I was just going to tell you a delivery came for you."

"Oh! But we aren't scheduled for any this morning."

"Not a medical delivery." His eyes were too bright and animated, and his smile was weird. What was happening?

She followed him out to the front and gasped when she saw the bouquet of lilies and hydrangeas. "Is that for me?" she asked.

"Delivery guy assured me he hadn't made a mistake. I asked," Dr. Brakeen teased. "All your years here and I've never even seen a boy pick you up for lunch, and now you're getting flowers? This one must be special." He winked at her and disappeared down the hallway toward room four to check with a patient.

Daylen had sent her flowers? Her heart was so damn full right now, she didn't know what to do with herself.

She leaned over and sniffed the bouquet. Lilies weren't really her flower, and neither were hydrangeas, but for personal reasons. But still! He'd sent flowers. He could've sent her a beef jerky bouquet and she would have just as many butterflies flapping around her stomach right now.

She plucked the card from the bouquet and sank into her chair as she ripped it open.

Obviously, Daylen would say something sarcastic and funny in the card, and she would keep it forever and ever because all of a sudden, she and her inner fox were crushing on that boy so hard, and...

She frowned as she read it.

Den. Can I call you Den? It sounds like a pretty pet name. You didn't respond after I was honest with you about the other prospects, but I have a confession. I made that up. I wasn't really talking to anyone else, I just said that so that it would possibly make you more interested in me. Or competitive with the other prospects, and you would put more effort into pursuing me, perhaps. I think I made a mistake with that. This is my apology. It's only you I'm interested in talking to. Please text me back.

Bartholomew

Oh…my…goodness gracious on cheesy toast!

Denver dropped the note like it was a hot-out-of-the-grease pork rind. This wasn't from Daylen at all.

The bell above the door rang out. Before this moment it had always sounded pretty, but right now? It was the ugliest sound in the world, because she was still reeling from the disappointment and uncomfortable feeling in the pit of her stomach and wasn't ready to face a patient.

Plastering on a smile, she moved the gaudy flowers to the side and froze.

Daylen was standing there leaning on the counter, his eyes pure spun gold, his arms all perfectly muscled against his tight black sweatshirt, a tan beanie on his head, and the hottest grin she'd ever witnessed on a man's face.

"H-h-hi."

He snorted. "H-h-hi back." He lifted up a

paper bag. "I'm paying you back for lunch at my work the other day." His eyes dashed to the flowers and back to her. "I have about ten minutes before I have to head back." He glanced again, and the smile faded a little. "Are those for you?"

"Uuuuuhhh, yes. But admission, I thought they were from you."

Daylen straightened up and glared thoughtfully at the flowers. "If I was going to give you flowers, I wouldn't give you your least favorite kind."

Now she was paying attention. "Oh yeah? And why are those my least favorite flowers?" Yep, this was a test.

"Because you tried to grow hydrangeas for two summers and you could never get the PH of the soil right. Their color kept fading, and you got mad at them and called them the devil's flower."

"Okay, hot boy, now I'm really curious. If you got me flowers, which ones would they be?"

"Weeds," he deadpanned.

"Thanks a lot," she muttered.

"I'm serious. I would get you a bouquet of those dandelion flowers. You used to blow the seeds everywhere and make wishes when we were kids. I think you ruined like thirty-seven yards in this town. I don't even know how you did that, because they aren't common here, but you always seemed to find them."

She laughed in surprise that he'd remembered such a silly memory. She still had a soft spot for dandelions.

"Who sent it?" he asked softly.

She handed him the note that came with the bouquet and waited for him to finish reading. His face stayed perfectly controlled the entire time, and then he put it back in the small envelope and asked, "Bartholomew who?"

She hadn't missed the small snarl at the end though. "I'm not giving you a last name, silly wolf. I know where that would lead, and that poor man doesn't even know you exist. This is the one my parents want me to give a chance to."

"For an arranged pairing?"

She nodded.

"Because you have responsibilities?" he asked, voice still soft.

Another nod.

"But you thought this bouquet was from me?"

Another nod.

"Why?"

"I guess because I wanted it to be from you."

He chewed the side of his lip and stared out the window for a few moments, and then relaxed and handed her the bag lunch. "It's ham and cheese, no mayo. Just meat and cheese."

Her favorite sandwich. Daylen had remembered.

He turned and walked toward the door.

"Are you mad?" she asked.

"No." He gave an empty laugh and shook his head as he pushed the door open with his back. "Of course not. I don't have any claim on you, Denver. We're just friends."

Those three words stung her. They hit like a slap on cold skin.

"I would rather have dandelions," she called as the door swung closed.

Outside, he froze with his back to her, his shoulders tense. He gave her the profile of his face, and his cheekbones were sharper, his jaw clenched. He turned slowly and he felt so far away with the glass door between them.

She stood and placed the bouquet of flowers right on the edge of the counter and mouthed, "I don't want these."

Daylen scratched the back of his head roughly and pulled the door open, and damn, that bell's song was back to being beautiful. He strode to her, made his way right around the counter, gripped the back of her neck gently, and kissed her lips. It was short, deep. He pulled away and rested his forehead against hers, and then said, "I don't know what I'm doing."

"Yes, you do," she murmured. He knew. He knew he was wrecking her heart and his. He couldn't help it, just like she couldn't help it.

"Tell him you're taken," he said, a growl tainting every word, and the fine hairs lifted on her arms.

She rolled her eyes closed and smiled. "Okay."

Daylen eased back and straightened up, arched up his eyebrow. "Yeah?"

Denver nodded, and tried to stifle her smile. Oh, she knew exactly what she was agreeing to. "Yes." She pointed to the flowers. "Can you take those out with you?"

"Yes ma'am," he rumbled in the sexiest voice she'd ever heard. "I'll see you tonight, Denver Mosley."

"Tonight?"

"I'm taking you out."

"It's Tuesday."

"And?"

"I sing on Tuesdays."

He lifted his chin higher into the air. "Good. I'll feed you beforehand. Do you mind if I watch you sing?"

Butterflies, butterflies, butterflies. "I don't mind at all. Pick me up at seven."

He gave a nod, gripped the vase of flowers in one hand, and made his way out of the office again.

After he drove off, Denver relaxed back into her chair, her cheeks on fire. He'd just asked her on a date. Right? He'd asked her out and told her to let Bartholomew know she was off the table.

Why did this make her so unbelievably happy? Why was her fox practically bouncing around inside of her with giddiness? She'd never felt like this in her entire life! How could any single feeling top this?

She'd always seen Daylen, but never this clearly.

With each passing day, it felt like perhaps the man who matched her had been Daylen all along.

SIXTEEN

Denver had made a misstep.

"Oh no, oh no," she murmured in horror as she looked at her reflection in the mirror.

A knock sounded at the door, and gosh-dangit! Daylen was early.

She looked like a carrot!

"Just a minute!" she called in sheer panic. He couldn't see her like this. He couldn't! He would never want to bone her!

She needed to put some clothes on. Possibly all the clothes she owned and also a ski-mask!

Denver flew into her bedroom and yanked a

bunch of pants out of her drawers, but paused. What if the orange stuff got on her clothes?

Daylen called from the front door, "Hey, are you all right? You're breathing really hard."

Yeah, well, that's how she panicked. "I made a mistake!" she drawled out, heartbroken.

"I'm coming in."

"Okay, but you have to swear not to laugh."

His footsteps sounded down the hallway, and her door creaked open. "Why would I—" Daylen's eyes went wide, and he pursed his lips tightly closed.

"You're laughing with your eyes," she grumbled.

"What did you do?" he murmured, touching her bright orange skin with his fingertip. He studied his hand. "Did you paint yourself?"

"I used self-tanner, okay?" She kind of wanted to cry, but more of her was just angry and trying not to laugh-sob.

A chuckle escaped his chest and she yanked away. "It's not funny!"

"It's kind of funny."

"I look like a naval orange."

"I love oranges." He couldn't even say the stupid words without laughing.

"Daylen! I did this for you! And now I'm embarrassed, and you're never going to let me live this down."

"I don't know what you're talking about," he muttered, but he was holding up his camera to take a picture.

She shoved his shoulder. He snickered and pursed his lips again. Now his shoulders were shaking.

"I even did my face," she said, pointing to her orange cheeks.

"Yeah, but not evenly."

Denver rolled her head back and closed her eyes, pouted out her bottom lip. "I'm supposed to sing tonight."

"Just go take a shower and wash it off."

"It lasts seven to ten days."

"Hahahaha," he belted out. He tried to stop

laughing, but failed. He was curled up, clutching his stomach on her bed as he cracked up.

"I hope you puke from laughing." She tried to say it grumpily but now she was giggling a little bit too. How could she not? His laugh was utterly contagious.

"Why did you dye your skin orange?" he punched out through laughs.

"Because it's the end of winter and my pasty skin hasn't seen sunlight in months. I'm whiter than the snow outside, and I don't know what I'm doing with my life! I got excited about tonight and then had a few hours to kill to do some self-care, and then I got a little nervous—"

"Nervous?" he asked, sitting up. "What for?"

"Because it's you! I'm hanging out with you and it's different now. I thought I would pour myself one glass of wine to settle down, and I drank that in the shower while I was shaving myself smooth as a naked mole rat. Then I remembered I had a self-tanning kit I bought a long time ago and never got around to using, so in my wine fog and nervousness I thought tonight was the perfect time to try it for the first time ever! I'm so dumb, Daylen!"

"Pumpkins are my favorite Halloween decoration."

"Aaaaaah!" she yelled dramatically as she flung herself backward onto the bed.

"Look, it's probably fine. You just look extra bright because of the white towel you're wrapped in. And this lighting in here is probably warm, so maybe it'll be fine when you dress in a different color and come out into the living room. Plus, I know how much you love makeup because you are the girliest creature I've ever met in my life, so I'm sure you have some face shit that will cover up all the streaks. On your cheeks." He grinned. "Your streaky cheekies."

"Yes! It'll probably be fine! It'll be great. Just some makeup and maybe a nice tan shirt and better lighting." She liked when he was positive and came up with solutions.

He let her have some space to get ready, and

she did so at double-speed.

And when she came out, filled with hope, she did a little twirl in the living room in front of him.

Daylen was sitting on the couch with his lips pursed into a thin line, and he was trying not to snort.

She caught a glimpse of herself in the full-length mirror by the door, and nope, the different lighting hadn't made a difference at all. Her makeup had though. She had a porcelain-white face and a bright orange neck and chest. The color changes looked especially bad against her fitted, light-brown dress and cognac-colored heeled boots. She looked like a Creamsicle. "That's it, I'm not going."

Daylen was back to not hiding his laughter again, and it made it hard for her to stay serious. A little giggle escaped her.

Daylen laughed harder.

She snorted and a laugh crawled up the back of her throat.

Daylen flopped over on the couch, cracking

up.

And now she was doubled over laughing, trying not to pee herself. It went on and on, until tears trailed down her white makeup and made orange streaks. And then Daylen punched out the words, "Streaky cheekies," again and she fell to the floor laughing.

He crawled over to her, his face red, and laid beside her as they kept getting pulled into waves of giggles.

It took a long time to settle, and for the final waves to die off. But when they finally did, he laid right beside her, and slipped his hand around hers. "You're pretty even when you are orange."

Awwww. She rolled over onto her side and squeezed his hand with both of hers. "That was sweet of you to say."

"I would still fuck you."

"You would?" she asked in a squeaky, mushy voice.

"I mean, I would have to close my eyes—"

She kicked him softly with the toe of her boot. "Stop it."

"Or turn off the lights."

Denver pouted. "You are hurting my self-esteem."

"No one on this planet or the next could hurt your self-esteem, Denver. You know I'm just kidding."

"Probably," she said at the same time as him, because he always said that after he said, "Just kidding."

The smile dipped from his lips for a moment. The laughter faded from his eyes and was replaced by a spark of intensity. "You know me."

She nodded and let him hear the truth in her voice as she whispered, "Better than anyone."

Daylen slid his hand to her waist, and then dragged his touch down her hip to the hem of her dress. He hesitated there, but she didn't stop him. As he dragged her dress up her leg, he trailed his fingertips against her smooth skin.

"Did you really shave for me?"

"Mmm hmm."

"Everywhere?" he asked in a husky voice.

Her heartbeat was out of control right now. Shaking just a little, she reached down and gripped his hand, then guided it between her legs. She wasn't wearing any panties.

"Fuuuuuuck," he whispered as he felt her smooth sex.

He pressed his fingertip right against her entrance and teased her, massaged around it. Denver rolled her hips toward him, pleading.

He scooted closer and leaned in, kissing her slow and deep as he slid his finger in up to his knuckle. The long, low growl in his throat was the sexiest thing she'd ever heard, and her fox answered softly.

He smiled against her lips and pulled his finger from her, then dragged his hand up her dress to her bra and cupped her breast. Denver moaned and arched her back, leaning into his touch.

"Noisy," he growled against her neck. *Nip.*

Nip. Bite. "I love when I know what makes you feel good."

"That feels good," she whispered, grabbing his hand and pressing it more firmly to her breast. "And this feels good," she said, dragging his hand back down between her legs. "And this…" She cupped his stone-hard erection through his jeans. "This feels good to me."

Daylen rocked his hips against her hand and let off a helpless sound that made her wetter in an instant.

She unfastened his jeans and pushed them down his hips, and he slid his finger into her again, stroking her deep as she met his movements.

Denver gripped his unsheathed cock and slid her grip down it, reveling in his murmured curse. Oooh, she could make him feel good.

She rested her knee on his hip, opening the apex of her thighs for him, tempting him, teasing him.

His kiss found her lips again and it was

harder now, his tongue thrusting deeper, his teeth biting her bottom lip harder between strokes. She was completely lost in him— moaning, writhing, begging. He moved his hips closer by an inch, and then another, and another.

Please, please, please.

The second his swollen cock touched in between her lips, she moaned out his name, and Daylen was done playing. He rolled her onto her back smoothly and gripped his dick, then slid it right into her. There was no easing it in, and she hadn't wanted that. He pushed deep into her, and Denver cried out as she arched her back against the floor.

He peeled off his shirt, pulled her dress over her head, and then lowered down so that their hot skin could touch. Everything was on fire in the best way.

Their friction was flames and gasoline, and he held her hands over her head as he bucked into her. She came fast and panted for a few more strokes, and then he started building pressure in her body again. How was this possible?

"You're not done yet," he murmured against her ear. He slowed down and slid into her deep, thrusting shallowly, staying right on that sensitive nub that was supposed to still be recovering.

The smooth pace he set pushed her into another orgasm fast, and she panted out his name over and over. What was happening to her body right now? He was consuming her completely, playing her like an instrument, commanding her fealty without words.

"Good girl," he rumbled against her ear, then nipped at her earlobe as he pulled back, and eased back into her. "I like when you come. I like when you're gripping my dick like this."

And she fa-reaking loved when he talked to her like this. Holy. Hell. She was so turned on. "You gonna give it to me?" she whispered against his ear.

"Do you want to take it?" he asked, his lips against her neck. *Bite. Bite.*

"Please," she begged, already *so* close again.

A few more hard strokes and her body imploded again, only this time, she wasn't alone. Daylen grunted and pulsed heat into her.

Every nerve ending in her body was tingling with pleasure, so she didn't really react to the bite. It was shocking. It should've hurt, but it didn't hurt at all. It tingled, and warmth trickled down the side of her neck as the scent of iron filled the air.

Daylen dragged out every last pulse of their releases, and then he gripped the back of her neck and rested his forehead on the side of her face, covering her body completely with his. "Do you understand?" he murmured quietly.

Denver clung to him like a life raft, her nails digging into the skin of his back as she tried to control her whirling mind. The fox was going insane with excitement.

Voice shaking, she said, "I know what that means."

"Are you okay?" *With the claiming mark.*

209

Those words remained silent, but she could hear them clear as day.

"More than okay."

A soft growl rattled from his chest to hers, and an excited set of yips escaped her. Daylen's body reacted with a humming vibration that rattled his entire frame.

"Can you Change?" Daylen's voice was strained. "I think I need you to Change."

"Yes!" She needed to. The fox was coming out of her whether she wanted it or not!

He pushed up and flung open the door, and then he fell to his hands and knees on the porch. He groaned in pain as the snapping of his bones cracked like fireworks into the night.

Oh, it was going to be a bad one for him. Oh no, oh no.

How long had it been for him? How long?

Her Change took seconds, the fox ripping out of her skin faster than she ever had before. Disoriented, Denver fell to her belly on the cold wooden boards of the front porch. Daylen's face elongated, and he snarled a pained sound as he fell to his side.

She wanted to help! She needed to help him! He was hurting!

Denver crawled to him, belly low, tail tucked, her black nails scratching across the boards. *Come out, Wolf. Come run with me.*

She let off her yips, over and over, loud and pleading. *Come out! Come out of him!*

The wolf shredded Daylen coming out of him. Just destroyed him, and her heart hurt to watch it. They were at war, Daylen and his wolf, and she didn't understand why.

Wolf was black, with a smattering of chocolate brindling through his coarse, thick coat. He had a patch of white on his chest and paws the size of her entire head. As he stood to his full height, glowing gold eyes trained on her, she had a moment of terror. They'd never Changed together.

Werewolves were crazy.

It's me!

He moved with a predator's grace as he came to stand over her. She'd always known he was dominant. He was a Hoda. He came from a long line of monsters. Lying here exposed, at the mercy of him, Denver felt the first trill of fear she'd ever had around Daylen.

He was different than she'd imagined. Bigger. More powerful. He sucked up every molecule of oxygen, left her lungs depleted and screaming for air.

She lay there frozen, unable to move as he lowered his enormous head to her neck.

He licked her there, where she'd been given the claiming mark.

He licked it, and she drew in a deep breath as the weight lifted off her. Seconds dragged on as he cleaned her broken skin, and with each breath she relaxed, until she was melted into the floorboards with her eyes closed to the world.

Wolf was taking care of her, and now something strange was happening. It was as if this thin, invisible rubber band was forming between them. It was elastic, stretching as he stood to his full height and trotted down the stairs, then through her snowy front yard. He paused at the edge of the woods.

The band had stretched tight, and it felt better when she followed him.

And through that band...that bond...she could get a feel for what he was experiencing.

Right now, her entire body was being filled with relief that didn't belong to her.

It had been a long time since the wolf had been out.

A feeling of gratefulness followed. Gratefulness for her. She'd pulled the wolf out of darkness, but she didn't understand how.

Excited by his emotions, she bounded through the yard and got the zoomies. She had to speed three laps around him before her body would slow down. Denver hopped up high and landed in front of him, her front legs flat against the snow, her butt up in the air, her tail wagging slowly.

The big black wolf was perfectly still, his emotionless eyes on her, his ears erect.

Maybe he didn't know how to play. Maybe no one had taught him how to—

Wolf took off like a bullet out of a gun. For a moment, she was stunned by his sudden speed before she caught on. He did know how to play!

Another echoing yip, and she bolted after him. *Here I come!*

There was nothing like running full-speed in this body. Everything was sharper. The world slowed down, and this form was completely comfortable with speeding up. She could jump and duck and dodge every branch that reached for her. Her instincts were insane in this body. She could hear and see everything, and she'd never been more thankful for that, because she was getting to experience pure joy from Wolf. He was running all-out too.

She knew where he was taking her when they were about a mile away from Promise Falls.

This had been their secret swimming spot

when they were growing up. By the bench, with the old rope swing that hung out over the water. Daylen had hung that there when they were ten. Two weeks ago, she'd thought they would never be at their spot again, and now look at them. Changed together and running straight for it. And she had his claiming mark! His claiming mark! Wolves were allowed to give it to one female in their lifetime. They were allowed to bite one, and he'd chosen her!! Aaaaaaah! EEEEEEeeee! Ahahahahaha! Today was the best day ever.

For the rest of her life, no day would be able to top this one.

For the first time ever, she felt completely whole and excited for the future.

SEVENTEEN

"I'm going to go say hi to Lyndi," Denver said, squeezing his hand before she released it.

"See you soon...pumpkin." He couldn't help snickering as she swatted his arm.

"I hate that pet name, pick another one...pumpkin fucker."

"Hey, orange is the sexiest color," he called out as she sashayed away toward the bar.

Little vixen. He took a seat at the table in the far corner and pulled out his phone to do something he'd been thinking about all day.

He connected a call he never thought he

would be interested in.

Stark answered on the second ring. "If you're dying, call someone who cares." Click.

Daylen pulled the phone away from his ear and stared at the screen as it faded to black. That motherfucker had hung up on him.

His phone rang, and Stark's name came across the caller ID.

"Pretty sure you aren't supposed to hang up on your Alpha, asshole," he snarled.

"Yeah, I just realized that. What do you want?"

Daylen let off an irritated sigh. This had been a mistake. "Look, I asked Denver if I should call the guys and see if any of them want to come back to the Pack now that Tessa is out."

"Yeah? And what did Denver say?" Stark sounded bored.

"She said Pack business is something me and you and Marsden need to figure out."

There was a beat of heavy silence. "You're asking me what we should do?"

"Yep. Against all better judgment, I'm asking a delinquent, last-chance, crazy-ass, unhelpful, immature—"

"Fuck them," Stark interrupted.

"Yep," came a voice in the background. "Fuck them."

"Is that Marsden?" Daylen asked.

"Yeah. We're having a bonfire night in your front yard. We stole the whiskey your dumbass tried to hide above the fridge. We would invite you, but you've been a little busy boning the fox."

"Stop stealing my shit, Stark," he growled. "And stop hanging out in my fucking front yard. I told you to move your stupid tent somewhere else."

"But you didn't say it like an order, so I figured secretly you wanted me to stay."

Daylen pinched the bridge of his nose and counted to three before he responded. "I super don't want you squatting on my front lawn, and what do you guys mean by 'fuck them'?"

"Those douche-canoes bounced, Daylen. They

left, and they made it look easy. Have they even texted to see if power has passed to you yet?"

Daylen chewed the side of his lip and watched Denver order some drinks from the bartender. "No. Not a single text."

"Those aren't the soldiers you want in your army, man. We veto bringing back the Pack. We are the Pack. Any new members have to be that—new."

He scratched his two-day scruff in agitation that he was taking this seriously. Stark had always been a wolf in it for himself, and that was all. Daylen had lost his mind asking his advice. "We need numbers. Three wolves do not a Pack make. We will have every Pack in the northern states up our asses in two months, tops, once they find out this territory is defended by three."

"Four," Stark quipped. "We have a fox, too. She's super scary." The sarcasm in his tone was truly obnoxious.

"Forget it," Daylen muttered, and went to disconnect the call.

"Wait," Stark said.

"What?"

"I like the fox. I mean for you."

Daylen frowned. "What do you mean?"

"I said what I meant, you fuckin' ferret, don't ask me stupid questions."

Talking to Stark was exhausting. "Do you want to come out to the bar or not?"

"What?"

"I said what I meant," he repeated Stark's words in a snarl. "We didn't celebrate our new fucked up Pack the other day, so...Denver is singing at Zaps tonight. I'll buy you boys a round."

There was a loaded silence, and then a muttered, "We'll be there in half an hour," before Stark hung up on him. Again.

He'd opened up and talked to Denver on the way here about the Pack and his worries over being in a leadership position, and she'd laughed. Laughed. Straight-up laughed at him and told him he would be fine, and she'd been so confident he'd believed her. And she pointed out something about Stark and Marsden that he hadn't realized before.

Tessa had kicked him out of her Pack a dozen different times, and always, always, the next day he would see Stark and Marsden. Never together. They would show up while he was running errands, or come up with something they needed from him, or sometimes Stark would just show up at whatever bar he was drowning his sorrows in and start a fight.

Denver said she thought they were finding ways to check up on him.

And as he sat here, spinning a round paper coaster slowly in his hands, other things struck him. Memories the wolf was dredging up. Stark always showed up looking like hell after Daylen got booted from the Pack. Black eyes, broken nose, clawed to hell like he'd fought everyone the night before. And fuck, maybe he had.

Stark and Marsden were always, always the first two hands that lifted in the air when the

Pack voted to reinstate him. His own brother didn't always vote for him to come back. And his mother sure as hell didn't, but she gave the Pack power enough to let him back in.

Maybe Stark and Marsden had quietly been the only ones who had seen value in him.

Or maybe they just liked picking fights, who knew.

He was going to have to figure out how to draw in some more wolves for this crippled Pack, and soon. But not tonight. Tonight, he was going to take a breath and enjoy a night with Denver, and try not to kill the boys.

She'd dragged the wolf out of him.

She'd really done that.

He didn't know what kind of magic a woman had to possess to drag a monster out of a canyon and ask him to heal, but he was going to find way to pay Denver back. He didn't know how, but he would.

Tonight was the first night in a month that he didn't feel like there was a boulder sitting on top of his chest.

She wore the brightest smile as she sauntered up to the table with his beer of choice in hand and a water for herself. Daylen stood and pulled her chair out for her, then pushed it in when she sat. She was chattering about something Lyndi said in the back, but it was so damn hard to pay attention to her words when he was mesmerized by the lips that formed them.

Her eyes were still bright from her Change, but muted enough that she looked mostly human. She wasn't having to wear sunglasses in here like he was.

Speaking of, she leaned forward and pulled them off as she chatted. Just smoothly and easily pulled the sunglasses from his face and then grabbed both his hands in hers. Her dark eyebrows arched prettily with animation as she spoke. Something about Lyndi planning a birthday party for her mate and inviting both Denver and Daylen. It was a nice gesture. Lyndi used to hate him.

Her parents were going to be the real issue. And Tessa. That she-wolf would rip out the throat of anyone she saw as being in her way.

Those were concerns for tomorrow though. Daylen would fix all that. He had to, because it was necessary to his existence that he make a safe, big, happy life for Denver. This was the first time he'd felt like that about anyone, but she was here, looking him straight in his eyes, smile genuine, curls bouncing with her talking, his claiming mark on full display like she couldn't be happier about it.

She'd patted makeup all over her face and neck to cover the orange, but the claiming mark? She'd left it bare and angry looking. It was healing slowly, as claiming marks did.

Silly girl. None of the humans here would understand the importance of it, but on the other hand, he loved that she was proud of it.

Did she even see the scar on his face now?

He didn't like mirrors much anymore, but he was just fine with his reflection in Denver's eyes.

Daylen looked different there. He didn't look much like a ghost anymore.

He was a beer and a half in when the boys showed up. They took seats at the table and verbally jabbed at Denver, but she took it like a champ and gave digs back to them. They were easy laughers in this environment. It was neutral territory. Daylen was mostly quiet, just watching the rapport between them. Even Lyndi came and joined them for a few minutes before Denver had to go make sure her guitar was tuned.

Lyndi watched Denver head to the stage, and there was a lingering smile on her face as Denver turned twice to wave to him.

"Our parents are going to be a hard win," she said without looking at him.

"I'm gonna talk to them."

She inhaled deeply and slid her attention to him, her arms locked against the back of Denver's empty chair. "They're going to have a big problem with that mark on her neck."

Stark and Marsden's conversation died to

nothing. They both went still and the air grew heavier.

Every table in here was full and the noise had been overwhelming before she'd said that, but with her words, the rest of the bar seemed to fade away.

Daylen leaned forward on his elbows, his eyes on Denver as she took the stool in front of the microphone and arched her neck as she plucked a few notes on her guitar.

"I'm going to take care of her," he promised.

"I know. You always did. I think that's what scared us so much. When you left, you took part of her, Daylen. It was hard for us to watch her light go out over the last two years." She straightened her spine and said, "It's good to see her again. You're lucky, but so is she. I can be there to talk to the parents if you guys want. I'll back you up."

Whoa. In a dozen years, he would've never seen this kind of support coming. "Thank you."

"Yep. Okay, I'm going to get back to work. One

of our servers called in, so I'm working this whole section now that Marian is leaving. I'll get another round of beers started. You boys be good tonight," she said, pointing at Stark and Marsden. "No fights, no breaking windows, no smashing furniture."

"We would never," Stark said in fake offense. They had definitely done that on multiple occasions.

Lyndi arched an eyebrow at the lie and hurried off.

"Hello, hello, how y'all doing tonight?" Denver's clear voice came over the speakers.

There were a few whoops and yells from the crowd, and the volume of the room came down a couple notches.

She grinned over at Daylen and gave him the cutest damn wink he'd ever seen. "I'm having a really good day today, anyone else having a good one?"

More cheering and whooping and God, she was good at this. Engaging, and confident talking to the crowd, looking around and meeting eyes. She'd grown into something so damn special.

"I bet it's better now that you have a beer in your hand," she joked with the loudest cheerer at one of the front tables.

"Hell yeah," the man called.

Her giggle echoed over the speaker system. "Good, good. I'm sure glad to hear that. I like when we have a happy crowd. I'm gonna keep it upbeat tonight, sound good? Y'all go dance if you feel like it." The entire time she was speaking she'd been strumming a tune, and the second she stopped talking, it picked up. She leaned back with this pretty curve to her lips and a faraway look in her eyes that made the bond pulse inside of his chest.

God, she was something to behold.

She sang the first few lines before Stark leaned over. "Dude, I didn't know the fox could sing."

Daylen had known it for a long time; he just hadn't known she could do it in front of a crowd until recently.

"When are you going to tell her?" Marsden asked.

Daylen's heart sank. That was the part he dreaded the most—the admission of what he'd done.

He didn't have an answer for Marsden, so he asked Stark something he'd been wondering instead. "When I got kicked out of the Pack, you always showed up wrecked the day after. I never thought about that until tonight and now I have to know. What happened each time I left?"

Stark made a clicking sound behind his teeth and took a long drag of his beer, bright blue eyes on Denver as she sang.

"I'm gonna keep asking until you tell me," Daylen assured him. "Might as well get it over with."

It was Marsden who spoke up. "He challenged Tessa for Alpha."

Daylen ripped his gaze away from Denver. Stark looked pissed, his features were tighter and his eyes brighter. "What?"

"You were better than both of those fucks anyways," Stark muttered. "Tessa held the whole Pack underwater, and Vager would've done the same thing. Like Momma Wolf, like son. Not you though. You were the apple that fell from the tree and rolled uphill."

"Why did you challenge for Alpha though?" Daylen asked. Stark was a brawler, but his dominance wasn't near enough to hold a Pack.

"So I could let you back in and give two middle fingers to Tessa. Obviously."

Holy. Shit. A shocked laugh escaped Daylen's chest. "You really aren't scared of anything, are you?"

"Wasps," Stark deadpanned. "I'm scared of wasps." He took another sip of beer.

Tessa and Vager could've killed him in any of those challenges, and he didn't give a single shit. Daylen threw his head back chuckling. "You really are crazy."

Stark looked utterly remorseless and was

cracking a grin now. So was Marsden.

"To the most fucked up Pack in existence," Daylen muttered, tipping his beer above the center of the table for a toast.

The boys clinked the glass bottlenecks of their beers against his before Stark said, "And you're king of the misfits now." He took a drink. "Lol to you choosing a fox mate. Maybe I can go find a pygmy goat shifter and Marsden can marry a blow-up doll, and we'll just make this a full-circle mixed bag of nuts. Make Tessa extra proud."

"Fuck her approval," Daylen told them. "I gave up trying to impress her a long time ago. If we're proud of what we've got, that's good enough for me."

And as Denver finished the last few lines of her song, he knew what he'd said was right.

For the first time, something felt *right*.

So he'd taken on a fox shifter mate, and he was down to a couple wolves, and one of them was tent camping in his front yard. He had a dozen problems that would be a torpedo in the hull of his ship tomorrow, but it was okay. He was going to make sure it was okay.

It wasn't just him anymore. He had people to take care of and it was awakening something good inside of him.

You're doing good, the wolf whispered.

And this time he knew he hadn't imagined it.

The man in him had always fought this role, but the animal? He was a Hoda wolf, born in fury and dominance, bred for leadership, with a protective streak that had been stifled for too long.

The animal was built for this.

"So are you," he murmured to the wolf, and hoped he understood.

EIGHTEEN

The *drip, drip* of the melting snow from the roof made Denver's heart expand with readiness for warmer weather. It had been a long winter. Two years of winter, perhaps, but Daylen had brought the sun back with him.

Outside the rustic antique store, the snow was nothing more than slush on the ground. It would be completely melted by tomorrow, and in a week's time, if they had gotten through the late-winter storms, little green shoots of grass would be popping up everywhere. Maybe even a couple of dandelions.

She circled an old butter churn and tried to imagine if it would look good in her house, or as a decoration for Daylen's cabin. Over the last couple of weeks, she'd been slowly looking for things to replace the ones she'd burned.

She had the day off but Daylen was busy, so she was enjoying a self-care day. She'd gotten her hair cut, had her nails done, and was now shopping. Thankfully, the orange had faded from her skin and left her looking bronzed, and today she was feeling like a million bucks. That probably had something to do with the fact that she'd spent every night for the last week with Daylen. Their routine made her happy from her bone marrow outward. With each passing day he grew more dominant, confident, and more in control, but with her he grew more thoughtful, gentle, understanding, and patient.

Watching him come into his own was one of the greatest joys she'd ever known.

Her phone rang, and her heart rate kicked up to a gallop when she read Daylen's name on the caller ID.

"Helloooo, sexywolf," she murmured quietly, so she wouldn't bother the two older ladies looking at old paintings along the wall across the store.

"I have news."

"Good news?" Please Lord let it be good.

"Mostly. I talked to your parents."

"Wait, what?" she uttered, releasing the butter churn's handle from her grip. She made her way outside for some privacy. "Did you see them in town or something?"

"No, I called this morning and asked if I could come and talk to them. I'm just pulling away from their house to head back to work. Abel gave me an extra hour at lunch to talk to them."

What the heck? "Okay, clearly you are still alive, right? I'm not talking to a ghost?"

He chuckled and told her, "I'm alive, and I still have all my skin."

"Hang on, I need to sit down for this." The antique shop was built like a log cabin and was set in a large field. In the yard, there was extravagant landscaping set around a bench. Right now, there were no flowers, but the bench was dry enough from the sun. She took a seat and inhaled deeply. "Tell me everything."

"They're all right with us. Or they will be. They don't have a choice because I'm not quitting on you just to make room for someone they like better for you. I told them how I feel and the things I appreciate about you."

"Did my mom cry?"

"The whole time. Your dad chewed me up pretty good in the beginning, but I expected that. And in the middle, Lyndi knocked on the door. She sat right beside me and told her parents how unhappy her pairing was. I had no idea. I felt so freaking bad for her, but she was tough about it. Did you know she was going through that?"

Denver's heart dropped. "I had a feeling from some of the things she's said to me lately, but I wasn't for sure."

"Yeah, I think she could use more time with

you. She was pretty wrecked when she was telling your parents. I think she's leaving him. And she said you had done it right and found someone you wanted, who wanted you back, and that she would never wish anything but a love match for you. I just let her talk. At the end, your dad looked at me and said, 'We don't have a choice, do we?', and I shook my head and told him no. Just like I didn't have a choice. I had to love you, because that's what I was made to do."

Denver's face fell and her eyes burned in an instant with emotion. It was the first time he'd used the L-word. She swallowed hard and whispered, "I had to love you, too."

He blew out a breath. "It's so damn good to hear that. Say it again."

"I love you, too."

"Your dad shook my hand when I left and asked us to come to dinner on Sunday night. Your parents followed me out to my truck and right before I drove off, your dad asked, 'We heard you were Alpha now. Won't the Pack always have to come first?', and I told him, 'Denver is Pack.'"

Chills rippled up her arms and she sat up straighter. They hadn't talked about this stuff yet. "I'm part of the Pack? But I'm not a wolf. It's against the rules."

"I make the rules for the Pack now, Denver," he said with a soft sternness that dredged up the fluttering sensation in her stomach again. He did that a lot.

Daylen had grown into a good man.

He was going to make one hell of an Alpha for this territory.

It felt like every piece that had been missing or broken in her life was mending itself, and Daylen was a huge part of that.

She looked up to the tree line, and froze.

There, on the edge of the woods, stood a familiar woman. The she-wolf herself. Tessa.

"Day?"

"What's wrong?"

"Tessa's here."

"Where are you?" he asked, his voice going from tender to snarl in an instant.

"Jade's Junk, over in Fairplay."

She could hear the roar of his engine as he hit the gas. "Can you get to your truck?"

Denver glanced over to her Dodge across the parking lot. When she looked back at Tessa, she was standing ten yards closer.

"No," she said, standing slowly. "She's too fast."

"Fuck!" Daylen yelled. "Don't give her your back. You hear me? Don't turn around on her. Keep your eyes on her, and don't Change unless you have to. If you do, get somewhere she can't get to you!"

Tessa blurred to Denver and stopped eight feet from her.

"Is that my son?" she asked in a voice that was all wolf. "Tell him I said hi."

"Tell him yourself," Denver murmured, offering Tessa the phone.

The ex-Alpha slapped the phone out of her

hand and squared up an inch from her face. Tessa was older, more dominant, and more powerful. She was taller than Denver by four inches at least.

"Would you like to have a seat?" Denver asked, gesturing to the bench. "We should talk."

The fox inside of her wanted out. She was writhing inside of her to be released, but that would set Tessa off. She'd always been volatile.

Tessa cocked her head and her gold eyes landed on the claiming mark on Denver's neck, long healed into a silver scar by now.

"I knew he was stupid, but not that stupid. Is he really planning to put a fox in charge of a wolf Pack? That bench would make a better Alpha than you. That's what you always wanted, right? You were always right there, learning our ways, manipulating Daylen until he was useless to me. Wolves revere females, and you took advantage of that."

"You think I want to be Alpha? I didn't even know I could be a part of the Pack until five minutes ago. Perhaps you're the stupid one, Tessa. I know if I have two sons, I'll never choose a favorite and then spiral when one has to sit on a throne I cushioned for the other. I would make a better Alpha than you, but you know what? I would never, ever want that title, because it would mean something happened to Daylen, and he is everything. He is air. He is all I see, so I don't want to imagine the devastation of getting thrown into that position. I would rather die than be Alpha of this Pack, so go fuck yourself and all the opinions you have of me. They don't matter, just like you don't matter. The only opinion that matters to me is Daylen's. Your greatest shame, that you will always have to live with? Will be how badly you failed your sons and your Pack. Daylen is everything and you are nothing, Tessa. Daylen will be ten times the Alpha you or Vager could've ever been. I can't wait for the day to come when you realize the truth of that."

Tessa's face morphed with fury, and when

she curled her lips back, her teeth were elongating. "I came here to kill you, but killing is an easy thing. It's fast. There's no suffering, and I want you to suffer, fox. You love Daylen, don't you?"

"Yes," she answered, no hesitation.

The smile that drifted across Tessa's face was pure evil. "I could tell. I can smell it on you like a sickness. Love is weakness. It is a knife that will keep cutting you as long as you allow yourself to feel it. You've made a mistake in your choice of a mate."

"I haven't. He's mine, and always has been. I'm sorry you're angry over that, but—"

"He can't be your mate, fox. He's already chosen another."

Whatever she'd expected to come out of Tessa's mouth, it wasn't that. "He chose me."

"Did you ask him where he got that scar on his face?"

"Tessa, stop!" Daylen was yelling from far away.

Stunned, Denver looked over at the discarded cell phone. The call was still connected, and he could hear this? Tessa's awful, empty smile stretched wider as she realized the same thing.

"He Turned a *human*, Denver. You know the rules. It's the same for foxes and wolves. You choose one. You claim one. There is no second mate, which means you don't count. You're nothing but his whore. His real mate is in Montana, turning night after night into the wolf he put inside of her. A wolf that looks just like him. Black fur. Gold eyes. Oh, she's beautiful. For the rest of your life, you will live in the shadow of his real mate, a wolf he chose. He bit her on purpose. Turned her, on purpose. You will always be the extra, and you will never count."

The betrayal did feel like the cutting of a knife straight through her middle.

Daylen was yelling something. "Don't listen to her! Denver, don't listen! I'm on my way!"

Tessa was worse than a coyote shifter and could never be trusted, but even she couldn't disguise a lie. Every word that Tessa was saying was truthful, Denver could hear it in the clear tone of her voice. Inside of her, the fox grew angry and quiet with realization that they'd been tricked.

Daylen, the one they had trusted the most, had tricked them.

Tessa was laughing. "Your face," she huffed out. "I've waited all these years and I finally get to see this face."

The laughing. That awful cackling laughter was the soundtrack to her heart breaking, and it was too much.

Rage boiled through her blood, and before she could think, she rushed Tessa and cracked her fist across her face. The deep snap of a breaking nose didn't do anything to put her heart back together.

Tessa's head snapped back and she hit the ground, and Denver dropped on top of her, pounding her fists across her face.

She got three hits in before Tessa shoved her

off so hard, she folded against the bench and broke the wooden seat with a deafening crash. Tessa snarled and leapt through the air, landing on her before she could untangle from the splinters. The smell of blood filled the air. Hers? Tessa's? They fought to kill each other, growling and screaming, fists on skin, vicious kicks. She should feel the pain, right? All she felt was her chest exploding with betrayal.

Tessa fell to the side, her body contorting, and Denver shoved up to her feet.

"Don't you Change, you fucking coward. Fight me like this. Woman to woman. Don't give this to your animal, you fight me like this!" she roared.

Tessa's snarls were constant now. If she was too far gone, the people inside of that store couldn't see a Change.

Denver grabbed her hair at the top of her scalp and dragged her toward the woods.

Tessa grunted in pain and gripped her wrists to ease up the pressure. "Let me go!"

But something bad had happened to Denver's

insides. She felt very little. No pain, no exhaustion, no hurt, no remorse...only the burn of anger at everything that had been given to her, and taken, and given, and taken again.

These goddamn werewolves had pushed her and pulled her and broken her into this. With a snarl, she threw Tessa against a tree so hard the thick trunk shook.

Tessa catapulted off it and hit Denver like a torpedo, and the fight that followed would be a blur to Denver for the rest of her life. She didn't know how long they beat on each other, how long they tried and failed to kill each other...to break each other.

Exhaustion came before death.

Her arms shook and her legs wouldn't hold her, and Tessa was struggling with the same.

And there in the mud, on their knees, hair a mess, faces covered in swollen bruises and streaks of blood, there they found common ground.

Neither of them had anything left in them to

finish the job.

Breathing heavy, Tessa rolled her head back and offered her a bloody-toothed grin. "That was fun."

"Psycho." Denver stood on shaky, locking legs and swayed heavily. Her limbs weighed a hundred pounds apiece.

"You'll never be enough," Tessa called after her.

Denver turned and gritted out, "I'm enough for me. You can't take that away." She spat red on the melting snow, and wiped her split lip with the back of her hand. "You could never take that away from Daylen either. He grew despite you suffocating him."

"Yeah? You gonna forgive him?"

Denver gritted her teeth hard and pointed at Tessa. In a trembling, fury-tainted voice, she said, "Fuck all of you."

Tessa's empty laughter followed her out of the woods.

Her emotions collapsed on top of her the

second she stepped out of the tree line. Perhaps it was the adrenaline dump that depleted her, but a sob shook her body as she began to accept what she'd lost.

She'd been so stupid. A stupid girl. She'd thrown away a safe pairing with someone she would've never grown weak like this for. Tessa was right. Love sure felt like weakness now.

She'd trusted Daylen and he'd kept something huge from her. He'd given her this mark on her neck, and it was a lie. Tears streaked down her throbbing face as she clapped her hand over the scar on her neck.

She heard his truck before she saw it, stooped to pick up her phone from the ground, and limped faster toward her truck. She made it up into the cab by the time he hit the parking lot and skidded to a stop beside her.

She rolled her window down and told him, "Don't get out!" She didn't need this to be any harder than it already was.

His eyes were a blazing yellow color as he

rolled down his window. "Are you okay?" he asked.

Panting, Denver gripped the steering wheel in a chokehold and stared straight ahead. She needed to hear it from him, or she would always wonder "what if". What if she'd been tricked by the she-wolf, what if she'd made a mistake.

"Did you Turn a human?"

"Denver—"

"Yes or no, Daylen. Did you already claim a woman?"

"Yes."

"The scar on your face." She looked over at him, and his face fell in shock.

"You're hurt, Denver. Let me take care of you and I'll tell you everything."

"The scar," she repeated.

He slammed his head back on the headrest and now it was him staring straight ahead. "I got it the night I Turned her."

"What's her name?"

"It's not what you think—"

"Her *name*, Daylen." The name would make it real. She really existed if she had a name.

"Ruby. Ruby Daughtry."

She let the hurt slide over her like a blanket of fire.

The vision of him biting a human mate wouldn't have hurt like this if she'd found out a month ago. She would've understood. But now?

Tears streaked down her cheeks.

Now it felt like the end of her world.

"You're free, Daylen," she uttered brokenly before she rolled up her window and drove away.

NINETEEN

"Is she okay?" Denver asked Gary the Bartender.

He scrunched up his face and said, "Define okay," as he pulled the bar door open and let her in. Zaps didn't open for another couple of hours, but Gary had called her half an hour ago and said Lyndi was spiraling.

Now, Denver had never seen her sister "spiral", so she didn't know what to expect when she entered the dark bar.

Up on the stage, Lyndi was strumming her guitar, off-key since she'd never picked up an instrument in her life, and was crying out a song about heartbreak. Oh God.

Lyndi looked up, mascara streaking down her cheeks, and gasped. "Denver! My sister. My only sister."

"I thought you girls had more sisters," Gary whispered beside her.

"We have two other sisters. Is she drunk?"

"I can hear you, with my fox ears."

"That's enough, Lyndi," she called. Gary the human Bartender didn't need to hear about that.

Lyndi took a long drink of her cocktail and set it back on the floor, then began playing badly again.

"She's not even tipsy. I gave her a lemon drop two hours ago, and ever since then I've been giving her shots of Capri Sun in her drinks instead of alcohol. I think she just snapped."

"I have an alcohol problem," Lyndi sang into the microphone.

"I'll take it from here." She offered Gary a tired smile.

"Hey, are you doing all right?"

"Me? Oh, I'm always good."

"It's just...I'm not trying to be rude, I swear, but you look like you haven't slept in days and your eyes are all puffy. Have you been crying?"

Denver fought the blanket of numbness that threatened to slide over her shoulders again. The last few days had been rough, but Gary didn't need to know about her embarrassing love-life.

"I could use an ice water if you have time," she said, ignoring his observations.

Gary the Bartender nodded in defeat. "Sure thing."

"Lyndi, stop talking about your alcohol problem, you don't even drink very much."

"Well, I'm drinkin' today!" Her sister reached down and grabbed her sugary, definitely non-alcoholic, cocktail and sat on the edge of the stage to take another drink. "I'm thinking about being your back-up singer."

Denver hopped up and sat next to her on the stage, and gently took the guitar from Lyndi's hand. "What's going on, sis?"

"I did it."

"Did what?" she asked, already knowing the answer.

"I left him. I left him. I packed my things and I left. I told Mom and Dad I was done, and then I went home and he said one thing, Denver. He said one thing and I stood there staring at him, wondering how the hell I had gotten to that point. He was going off about how I never keep the house stocked with groceries for him, how that's my job and I'm always failing at my end of the bargain. I just stood there wondering when my value morphed from being a woman to being a servant, and I'm so unhappy. I have been for so long."

"Why didn't you tell me sooner?" Denver asked. "Why didn't you lean on me?"

"Because if you say 'I'm unhappy' out loud, you can't ignore it anymore. You have to face it. Saying it out loud makes it real." She dragged her tear-rimmed gaze to Denver.

Denver swallowed down her own emotion and hugged Lyndi up tight, because that's sometimes what a broken-hearted person needed. And truth be told, Denver needed it right now too.

"I know what I'm giving up," Lyndi whispered, "and I'm okay with it."

"What are you giving up?"

"One mate per lifetime, and I quit mine. But you know? I would rather be alone than feel alone with another person."

Those words pierced her heart, and she squeezed her sister tighter. "Everything is going to be okay. Those rules are stupid."

"Yeah, but I'm young. I have no kits. No fox will ever touch me again. I've failed."

"Then you'll find someone who doesn't care about those stupid rules, Lyndi. Your life isn't over."

And as she spoke them, the words were hitting her. The rules were stupid. It was the first time in her life she wished she wasn't a fox and

Daylen wasn't a wolf. She wished they were human, and claiming marks didn't exist, and they could just...be.

Lyndi sniffed and eased out of the hug. "You're throwing it away, Denver."

Denver frowned and canted her head, but Lyndi only stared at her clasped hands in her lap. "You blocked Daylen."

She huffed a breath and scooted a couple feet farther from Lyndi. "I didn't block him. I just turned my phone off. I needed a break."

"He's been calling and texting you. He cares."

"He also Turned a human, Lyndi. I don't want to be a man's second choice. I want to be a man's only choice."

Lyndi pulled something out of her back pocket and slid it across the floorboard. It was a half-burned picture of Denver, mid-laugh. Baffled, she plucked it off the ground and studied it. She remembered this picture. She'd burned it in the bonfire she'd made in Daylen's front yard.

"Do you know where I got that?" Lyndi asked,

her voice thick.

Denver shook her head.

"Stark stole it off Daylen's fridge yesterday. He's had it hanging there ever since the day you burned a bunch of his shit. Stark brought it to me and told me what had happened, but it's a lot right now, Denver. I'm going through my own shit, but I can't watch you throw a good life away. I would give anything to have a mate feel about me the way Daylen feels about you."

"He was with someone else," she whispered thickly, and fuck, here came the waterworks again.

Denver hung her head and two tears made dark spots on her jeans.

"Stark told me what happened."

"Why are you hanging out with Stark? He's bad news."

"He came here looking for you, dork. Asked me to give you a message."

"Fine, and what's the message?"

"Daylen is destroyed without you. You have

been ignoring his texts and calls, so he's trying to give you space because he's trying to be respectful, but it's killing him to stay away. Whatever Tessa said—"

"Was true! I could hear the truth in her voice."

"Whatever she said was twisted to fit the narrative she needed you to hear. It was a twisted truth, and she got exactly what she wanted. She got you to leave, but it was at an awful cost to you and to Daylen."

Why did her heart hurt so much lately? It's like she'd been ripped wide open and the wound was only getting bigger instead of healing.

Lyndi cupped Denver's cheeks, and she was spilling tears like crazy. "Tessa ordered him to Turn that woman."

No. No. Denver tried to deny it. Tried to shake her head no, but Lyndi wouldn't let her.

"My spiral is different. I'm going to be loud and awful and howl at the moon until I feel like I can breathe again. Until I feel hope again. But I know you, Denver. You will go quiet, just like you did the last two years, and you'll deal with your broken heart in silence. I can't watch that again. Not when you don't have to do this. You have a man who is wanting to catch you…you just won't jump."

"An order?" she whispered brokenly. "She could've destroyed him."

"She destroyed parts of him, but you're bringing him back. I could see it the night you guys were in here, and he dragged Stark and Marsden in here. They didn't get into a single fight that night, and you know what I saw, over and over and over?"

"What?" she asked shakily, because her heart felt like it would explode. Never in her life had Lyndi talked so openly to her.

"I saw you guys look at each other like no one else existed. Some people never find that in their entire lifetime, and you found it with the boy you've always known. Your love story stretches decades…and it's beautiful. It's a tragedy to let his past, or the things Tessa said, kill that story." She arched her eyebrows and released Denver's face, then wiped her mascara smudges with her sleeves. "Stop being a stubborn ape, and go put both of you out of your misery. Let him tell you what really happened. To him, Denver. Let him tell you what happened to him, and why he came back quiet like he did. And if it's bad? If he did bad? If he was imperfect? Listen with an open heart, because men don't move in a straight line. They improve, and then they get confused, and they go off-track, and then they are guided back to the right way with consequences. A good man will try to keep his path moving in the right direction. A bad one? He will enjoy being off-track, no matter the hurt he causes. Do you understand?" She placed her hand on her chest and leveled her with a look. "I found a bad one. You did not." Lyndi relaxed back and slurped the rest of her drink through the straw. "Now, if you don't mind, I have to get back to my spiral."

"Gary has been giving you shots of Capri Sun,

not vodka."

Lyndi's mouth fell open and she tossed an accusing look at Gary the Bartender, who was behind the bar washing glasses for the upcoming shift. "Traitor!"

He shrugged remorselessly. "We open the doors in two hours and I'm not working by myself while you sleep it off in the break room. Do you want another kiddie-drink, or nah?"

Lyndi glared for a few seconds and then gave her attention back to Denver. "I'm going home to clean up."

"Are you okay to drive?" Denver teased.

Lyndi shoved her in the shoulder and stood, then straightened out her T-shirt. "I think we need to have a discussion about me being your back-up singer though."

"Hell no. You sing like an injured hyena."

"Ha!" Gary the Bartender barked out.

"Kicking me when I'm down," Lyndi muttered as she pulled her jacket on and headed for the door.

"You won't be down for long," Denver
promised.

"I threw away my shot at a family, Denver.
This will be a decision that echoes through my
entire life."

"It feels like that right now, but not everyone
cares about our rules."

Lyndi's face went blank. "But...our
community..." she said carefully.

Denver finished for her, "Isn't the only
community."

Lyndi frowned thoughtfully to herself,
turned, and made her way out of the bar.

Denver looked back down at the picture of
her that Stark had stolen off Daylen's fridge. He'd
hung this up? He'd saved it from the fire and kept
it?

That was something.

Okay, Lyndi. She was listening. Hope felt so
much better than the awful empty feeling she'd
been consumed by over the last three days.

With purpose, Denver stood and jogged to

the door. "Bye, Gary the Bartender!"

"Still not my name," he called back with a smile in his voice.

She bolted across the parking lot and hopped into her truck, then fishtailed it out of the parking lot. She wanted to hear now. She was ready.

She just needed to get her phone from the house. She'd tossed it behind the dresser three days ago when she'd come home in such deep grief and Googled Ruby Daughtry. She hadn't posted on her social media pages in a couple of months, but she was gorgeous, and seeing her pictures had made Denver question herself. It had hurt her feelings and made her feel less-than, and she'd turned off the phone and thrown it out of sight so she wouldn't be tempted to go hurt her own feelings searching for Ruby Daughtry again.

She pulled to a stop at the red light in town, her brakes squealing. She tapped her fingers impatiently on her steering wheel. It had been torture living so close to the man she was most hurt by, but now she was grateful he was so close to her house. It made it really easy to pass her driveway and head farther up the mountain.

Who needed a phone when she could just talk to him in person? He should've been off work now, if he was working the early shift.

The last couple of miles up to his cabin took an eternity. The nerves had set in. Denver was just as vulnerable as she had been three days ago, after she'd fought with Tessa and found out that awful news. And now she was heading to another encounter that would hurt. It would.

But she had to dig in and learn to look past her anger, or she would never be okay. The fox would never be okay, because for her, Daylen was it. There wasn't another, and never would be.

She crept up to his house, but it looked different. The old, dilapidated gutters had been ripped off and replaced with new ones in the same color as the wooden house. New landscaping beds had been etched into the yard. A gravel parking lot had been created to the right, and Stark and Daylen's cars were parked side by side there. Stark's tent had been moved farther back to the tree line. The bonfire debris had been completely cleared and looked like it had never existed at all. The dog bed was gone from beside the front door, the porch was swept clean, and the lawn was coming in green. A pile of rotted floorboards sat to the left of the cabin. If she had to guess, he probably ripped out the flooring that had been damaged by that broken window letting the weather in.

The house looked great, and a pang of mixed feelings hit her as she remembered all the hours she'd spent here after he left, trying to fix it up for him in the little ways she knew how. She'd fallen in love with this house because it was the piece she had left of Daylen in the long two years he'd been making another life.

It shouldn't have hurt so much.

Perhaps she'd always loved him and she just

hadn't realized it.

The door opened and Daylen came out with a duffle bag slung over his shoulder. His head was downcast, and his lips were set into a grim line. He hadn't shaved in a while, and there was new scruff on his chiseled jaw. He looked good scruffy. Damn good.

He looked over at the tent, and then back down, and finally up at her. Daylen locked his legs and froze, his eyes blazing such a striking gold, she got trapped there in his gaze.

He looked utterly stunned. Daylen straightened his spine and let the duffle bag fall to his side.

Why was she crying? He hadn't even said anything yet, but just the open pain in his eyes was enough to rip her heart open more.

She pushed open the door and settled her feet on the damp ground.

"You're here," he said on a breath.

"I'm still angry at you."

He nodded. "I understand." He kicked at a

lump of grass with the toe of his work boot. "Did you get my messages?"

She shook her head. "I haven't read them yet. I just needed to disappear for a while. Figure myself out, you know? It's not like when I was a kid and I could just burn out my anger and come back and apologize. Now I try to be more careful."

"I know. You've changed so much. Me too, I guess."

Denver crossed her arms over her chest to ward off the chilly wind. "You moved the dog bed." Guess he'd already given up on her coming back.

Daylen tossed a glance behind him. "I don't want to soften things. I want to say them like they are and not be worried you'll run."

She didn't understand, so she just shook her head slightly and waited.

"I moved the dog bed inside, Denver. I don't want you sleeping out in the snow when you can be in there with me. I listened for your fox every night. I want you to be in there," he said, pointing to the cabin. "Not out here."

She couldn't. She couldn't hold his gaze, so she looked at the pattern of the young grass shoots, and bit her trembling lip to try and stop showing so much emotion.

"I hung a pair of bright yellow curtains in a bachelor pad, because they made me think of your favorite color. And I put in a bigger water heater so you can maybe take those long showers you love, if you ever get it in your mind that you can come back. I'm still building, Denver. I'm Alpha now. I didn't accept it until you made me feel okay enough to accept it. I'm going to do my best to build this Pack into something you can call home, when you're ready. Do you understand?"

She wrapped herself up tighter and nodded.

Daylen set the duffle bag down and approached slowly, hesitated, and then went down to a kneeling position so he could meet her downcast eyes. "Ruby is hard to explain, because

I don't quite know what happened myself."

"Did Tessa order you to Turn her?" she whispered thickly.

"Yes. She was convinced that Ruby was Vager's, because she had helped him while he was in jail. When Vager died, Tessa got attached to this...human woman who didn't want anything to do with our Pack, and in her grief, she tried to force her into the family."

"And she used you to do it."

He nodded. "The whole Pack voted on it. I was supposed to take on Vager's mate, because I was taking Vager's place. Everyone voted for me to take her, except for three people."

She guessed. "You. Stark. Marsden."

He nodded. "We lost the vote by a lot. The Pack was hurting, and it was being eaten up from the inside out. We'd just lost our future Alpha and our current Alpha was spinning out, and it destroyed us. It destroyed me. It destroyed Ruby's life. This?" He pointed to the scar down his face. "She did it with a crowbar, and I fuckin' deserved it. She fought, and I wanted to stop, but I didn't have control of my fucking body. Now every time I look in the mirror, I'm reminded of what I did, and how helpless I felt. All I see is a monster. But when I'm around you…" He swallowed hard. "You're the mirror I can look at. To you, I'm a better man. I'm the man I could be. I'm the man you believe in, and God, it was so addictive to just feel good for a little while. Like I was salvageable, you know?" He reached forward and gripped the back of her ankle. "You aren't some second choice, or any of the things Tessa said to you. I've been choosing you since we were kids." And then the Alpha of this territory tilted his head to the side, and exposed his neck to her. "I'm sorry for all the things I ever did to hurt you."

Denver covered her face with her hands as sobs wracked her body. Her knees hit the ground, and he wrapped her up tight. He dragged her into his lap and rocked her as she cried.

He pressed kisses to her forehead, her

cheeks, the top of her head, mumbling soothing words. "I'm still here. You're still here. Everything is okay. I'm going to make it okay."

It took her a few minutes to wear herself out, and she wrapped her arms around his neck and hugged the life out of him. His duffel bag sat there in the yard, and she asked, "Were you going to leave again?"

"Yes."

She pressed the sleeves of her sweatshirt to her damp cheeks and eased back to look up at him. "Were you going to come back?"

"Always." His eyes were rimmed with emotion as he studied her face. Daylen smoothed her flyaway tresses of hair behind her ear. "Our bond burns when I'm not near you."

"Where are you going?"

"Montana. Do you want to go with me?"

She sat up straighter. "Why Montana?"

"Because I need to face what I've done. I need to go back and give Ruby an apology, and dig into the part of me I'm not proud of. It's the only way

I can fix the wolf and be good enough to lead this Pack. It's the only way I can be good enough for you." He dried her tears with the pad of his thumb. Softer, he said, "Come to Montana. See the worst part of me. Meet Ruby."

He was asking her to see what he'd done and forgive him. He was exposing the part of himself that had changed the course of his life and almost ruined everything, and he was doing it for her—so she could see him at his worst, so she could appreciate how much he would grow.

Lyndi had said they looked at each other like no one else existed. That some people never found that in their entire lifetime, and that Denver had found it with the boy she's always known. She believed Lyndi now.

Her love story stretched decades...and it was beautiful.

He was asking her to do something hard with him, and really see him, and believe in him enough to stick around after.

Denver sniffled and nodded. "Okay."

TWENTY

Why was she so nervous? On the long road-trip here, Daylen had told her everything. Every brutal thing he and the Pack had been through over the past couple years. He'd painted a clear picture of exactly how it had been, including encounters with Ruby.

She'd called her work and asked for a few more days off, which Dr. Brakeen agreed to immediately since she had rarely ever asked for anything. Daylen was off for a few days too, and the trip here had been beautiful.

Just a last-minute out-of-state trip with a pair

of duffel bags, and the sun shining, and uninterrupted quality time. Already, her heart felt more settled and comfortable. Especially after hearing his side of things, and understanding the truthfulness of his tone as he admitted all the hard stuff.

She hated that any of this had happened, but she thought perhaps it was partly to credit for them finally seeing each other as something more than friends.

If his wolf hadn't been hurt, would he have ever realized she could fix the broken bits? And would she have realized how important he was if she'd never been invited into his vulnerable moments as he struggled to grow?

She didn't know, but she was a bright side kind of person, and if they had to go through this to finally, truly see each other, then it wasn't so bad. It was just another part of their story.

Still, seeing Ruby face-to-face had her heart rate kicked up a bit.

Daylen pulled into the parking lot of a

restaurant called The Beginning, and she smiled at the sign. Felt fitting. It was an old-timey eatery with an old grain mill out front next to a towering windmill. The porch had worn-out rocking chairs all down it, and a few groups of people were front-porch sitting outside.

"Maybe there's a wait," she murmured as he led her across the parking lot.

Daylen wrapped his big, strong hand around hers and squeezed it comfortingly. "Ruby and Divar are already in there. His truck is over there." He pointed to an old, burgundy-colored, jacked-up, rusted pickup truck parked along the curb. A trio of crows were perched on top of it.

"Who is Divar?" she asked.

He gave a private smile and told her, "You'll see." Daylen pulled a pair of sunglasses on, and she understood. His eyes were too bright gold to pass for human eyes right now.

"Are mine okay?" she whispered hurriedly.

"You are perfect." He leaned in closer and against her ear, he whispered, "You look so pretty today."

"Well, you're easy to please," she joked. Currently she was wearing skinny jeans, a pair of black low top Converse, a black tank-top, and a flannel. Her curls were down and wild. She'd thought about dressing up, because the thought of Ruby intimidated her, but she'd decided last minute to wear what was comfortable. Daylen had given her lots of compliments, so she figured she got it right.

Nervously, she wrapped her free hand around the inside of his elbow and bumped against him as he searched the busy restaurant.

"There," he murmured, twitching his head toward a booth in the back corner.

An auburn-haired beauty was talking animatedly to the barrel chested, silver-eyed silverback of a man beside her. Neither of them wore sunglasses, and when Ruby turned to look in their direction, Denver was struck by how similar her gold eyes were to Daylen's.

Daylen stood frozen next to her, but Denver

lifted her hand into the air and gave a little wave.

She didn't know what reception she expected, but the woman...Ruby...smiled and waved back.

Everything was going to be great.

She could feel the emotions humming from Daylen through the bond. Guilt was the biggest one. It was dark like a storm cloud, and bitter.

Desperate to help, Denver wrapped her arms around his waist and looked up at him. She grinned. "Come on. We'll do it together."

His Adam's apple bobbed low in his throat, and his lips curved up slightly. The smile didn't reach his eyes yet, but it would. She would make sure of it.

She moved first, leading the way to the table. Ruby and Divar stood to meet them.

There was a loaded moment she would never forget. Divar's stern focus was on Daylen, and Ruby's head was cocked, her eyes serious.

"I'm sorry," Daylen said, breaking the silence. "I'm so sorry."

Ruby's eyes dropped to the floorboards, and when they lifted again, they were softer. She stuck her hand out to Daylen. "Hi. I'm Ruby."

The look on Daylen's face, as Ruby started them fresh, oh the look. He huffed a relieved sound and nodded. His eyes sparked with vulnerability as he glanced at Denver, and then looked back to Ruby. He shook her hand, and twitched his head toward Denver. "This is my mate, Denver. Fox shifter."

There was no jealousy, no looking her up and down. There was nothing but a genuine grin and an offered hand. "It's nice to meet you, Denver." Ruby introduced the muscled, silver-eyed behemoth at her side. "This is my mate, Divar. Grizzly shifter."

Denver's mouth plopped open. "You're a Bane brother?"

"Nope."

"Oh okay, this is just me standing by a random grizzly bear shifter who isn't supposed to exist. I'm not scared. Are you scared?" she asked, pointing to Daylen.

"He ain't scared. We've fought before," Divar muttered. "I already ordered us a round of shots, because I'm not fucking doin' this sober."

Denver snorted, and Divar and Ruby took the bench seat across from them.

"Thank you for meeting me," Daylen told Ruby.

"It wasn't for you. I would've said no, except you told me you needed to be better for your mate. That stopped my anger and made me think. It made the wolf think." She dashed her gold eyes to Denver. "Mates are important. I've learned that they can be an anchor when you're spinning out of control." Divar slid his arm over her shoulders and she leaned in to his side naturally. To Daylen, she said, "I'm mostly here because I wanted to meet the woman who could tame a wolf like you."

Denver teased, "There's no taming him, it's a shit-show. I'm just along for the ride most days."

Ruby laughed a big, pretty sound. "I can't

even imagine. My wolf feels out of control most days. Divar keeps me steady."

"How did you two meet?" Denver asked them.

Ruby's look for Divar was so loving, it dumped a warm feeling into Denver's chest. "We sort of met because of Vager. We fought things at first, but I think it just took us a while to figure out that everything happens for a reason. What about you guys?"

"Oh, I've known this little fox since I was a kid," Daylen said quietly. He gave Denver a quick wink. "She's been annoying me for the better part of three decades."

Ruby frowned. "Then why? I never figured that part out. If you had your person, why Turn me?"

Daylen shook his head and ripped up the corner of a napkin. "It wasn't my choice. It was the Pack's vote. It was my Alpha's order."

Ruby's shoulders slumped. "Geez. Will the Pack come back for me?"

"The Pack is done. At least the Pack you

knew. Most of them left because of bad leadership, and I'm Alpha now." He lifted his gold gaze to Ruby. "I promise you and your people will never have trouble from me and mine again. If you need anything, call. If you get into trouble, call. If you need allies, call. I only have two wolves, and Denver now, but we'll grow. Plus," he said, with a teasing spark in his eyes. "We're crazy."

Divar chuckled, and cleared his throat to cover it. He couldn't hide the humor on his face though. "For real though, werewolves are fuckin' crazy."

The shots arrived and they ordered enough appetizers to feed a small country. And as Ruby lifted her little glass in the air, she made a toast. "To not hating you anymore, Daylen. And to learning to love what I've become. The wolf made me a better match for Divar, and you gave that to me."

Daylen slid his arm around Denver and pulled her in close against his ribs. His eyes were locked on hers when he said, "To things happening for a reason."

TWENTY-ONE

Stark was standing in the front yard with a homemade sign.

Now, she had very good vision on account of her fox, but Stark's handwriting was very bad.

"Welcomedome, asshats," she read out loud.

"I think it says 'welcome home, assholes,'" Daylen corrected her.

"Oh, my bad."

With a grin, the blond-haired giant turned the posterboard around. *You sick*, it read, but she was pretty sure it was supposed to say, *You suck*.

Aw, so sweet.

Marsden stood beside Stark with his hands shoved deep in his pockets, but he waved as Daylen parked the truck.

"This feels good," she said excitedly.

"What does?"

"I mean being back here. It was so fun getting a few days with you, but it feels good to be home."

Daylen grinned, and told her, "I can't believe I'm saying this, but I agree."

The trip had been good for them. They'd gotten to know each other on a whole new level, and she knew exactly what she wanted now.

Stark plucked another poster from the snow. This one read *Welcome to the back*.

"Welcome to the back?" she asked as she got out.

Stark frowned at his sign, then put it on the ground and yanked a marker from his back pocket and corrected it, then held it out again. *Welcome to the Pack*.

"Aaaaah," she said excitedly as she did a

weird little celebration dance over to him. Stark was dancing too, and Marsden rolled his eyes heavenward.

"Don't fight it, man," Stark told him. "Just go with it. You'll get more chicks that way."

"Oh yeah?" Marsden asked as they continued to dance. "Have you ever had a girlfriend?"

"Yeah, once. For like three weeks," Stark told him.

"Three weeks. Why would I ever take girl-advice from you?" Marsden asked.

"Because you know what they say about coaches. They don't have to play."

"Oh God, are you going to move your tent now? Everything is fine. We are official. Pack of four," Daylen said, coming to stand beside her.

"I was thinking of building a permanent structure over there," Stark said, pointing to the tree line to the right of his tent.

"I will kill you," Daylen assured him.

"Yeah, yeah, I get it, I get it," Stark said, holding up his hands in surrender. "You two wildcats want a few days to celebrate the honeymoon phase of your relationship. I will give you space."

Daylen's eyes narrowed on Stark. "You're moving?"

"Yes."

Daylen muttered, "Thank God."

"Deeper into the woods so I can bring girls here and you won't turn them off of my charms."

"What girl is going to want a night in a tent with you, Stark?"

"Bet I could get Lyndi in there. She's super vulnerable—"

"Stark!" Denver yelled. "No. You're being bad. Lyndi is off-limits."

"Amateur move," Marsden muttered. "Never tell Stark something is off-limits. You just gave him a challenge."

"I made us all hot dogs," Stark announced. "Over the open fire, because it's way better than cooking them in a microwave."

"You made dinner?" Daylen asked

suspiciously.

"Yes. To celebrate. We have four whole people in our Pack now. I knew you would forgive him," he said to Denver. "How many hot dogs do you want?"

"Four."

Stark arched his eyebrows up and looked impressed. "That's a lot of wieners—"

"Noooo," Daylen and Marsden drawled out in matching, tired voices.

Denver laughed and followed Stark to his campsite. Looking over her shoulder, she told Daylen, "I love wieners."

He snorted a laugh as he watched her go, and this was it. This was the moment that made all of the rest of her life make sense.

Hot dogs with three crazy werewolves in the front yard of the man she loved. Tomorrow would bring surprises, like it always did, but that was okay. She was okay.

From here on, she was a part of something. A part of this makeshift family that wouldn't make sense to anyone else but her. These boys had Daylen's back, and so she appreciated them. They were part of something important. They were a part of him.

Daylen had said he was trying to build her a home. As she looked from Stark, who was chattering as he ripped open a bag of hot dog buns, back to Marsden, who was chatting low with Daylen...and Daylen himself, his soft, adoring smile trained on her...she knew he'd done it.

He'd succeeded.

He'd made her a home.

And for as long as she lived, she was going to make sure he had a home, too.

THE FALL OF PROMISE

T. S. JOYCE

Up next in The Wolves of Promise Falls Series

The Rise of Promise (Book 2)

About the Author

T.S. Joyce is devoted to bringing hot shifter romances to readers. Hungry alpha males are her calling card, and the wilder the men, the more she'll make them pour their hearts out. She werebear swears there'll be no swooning heroines in her books. It takes tough-as-nails women to handle her shifters.

She lives in a tiny town, outside of a tiny city, and devotes her life to writing big stories. Foodie, wolf whisperer, ninja, thief of tiny bottles of awesome smelling hotel shampoo, nap connoisseur, movie fanatic, and zombie slayer, and most of this bio is true.

Bear Shifters? Check

Smoldering Alpha Hotness? Double Check

Sexy Scenes? Fasten up your girdles, ladies and gents, it's gonna to be a wild ride.

For more information on T. S. Joyce's work,
visit her website at
www.tsjoyce.com

Printed in Great Britain
by Amazon

15947459R00171